Fearless

ANNIE JOCOBY

BOOKS

Vinci Books

vinci-books.com

Published by Vinci Books Ltd in 2026

1

A CIP catalogue record for this book is available from the British Library.
Paperback ISBN: 9781036703059

The EU GPSR authorised representative is Logos Europe, 9 rue Nicolas Poussion, 17000 La Rochelle, France
contact@logoseurope.eu

By Annie Jocoby

Fearless

Chapter One

Dalilah

"Sorry I'm late," I said to Kyle, who was tapping his toes and crossing his arms as I rushed into the tiny changing room.

"Doll," he said, "you've been late a lot lately. What's going on?"

I swallowed hard, knowing that I really couldn't tell him the truth. Which was that I drank a few too many shots and ended up in the apartment of some guy in Queens. Considering that this art studio was located in SoHo, which was a considerable subway ride away from Queens, it was no wonder that I was a half hour late.

"Sorry," I said. "It won't happen again."

"Better not. You better be glad that you got that beautiful boy Seth taking care of your pretty little ass. Otherwise, you might be out on the street. Because one more tardy, and you're gone."

I bit my lip, knowing that he was absolutely right. I had

long since declared absolute financial independence from my parents, over their objections, and this part-time job modeling nude for art students was really my only source of income. Well, that, and my side gigs modeling for established artists in the Village. Between all of these gigs I made enough, just barely, to afford my studio apartment in SoHo.

Seth was much more established than myself. He was 21 and graduated early from Harvard and had taken his first job in the financial district. So he was making bank. Which he constantly threw in my face. Still, he more or less took care of me and made sure that I had groceries in the house. And the sex with him was pretty good, I guess. The high school rumors that were circulating about his Johnson did prove to be pleasantly true, which was a plus.

Kyle was still crossing his arms as I hurriedly changed out of my clothes and into my white robe. I hated to keep the class waiting, I really did. Quite frankly, I was embarrassed to be in that situation. But it did seem to be happening more and more frequently for whatever reason.

Seth knew about my extracurricular activities and seemed unconcerned about it all. "You do what you want, Dalilah," he had said. "As long as you keep doing that thing you do with your tongue, I'm good to go."

Permission having been granted, I had the freedom to do whatever it was that I wanted, within my budget, of course. And I took it. I was 20. If I had gone to college, I would be going to keggers and screwing random strangers, because that's what you do in college. That's what Alaina was doing over at NYU. So, I felt that I was somehow fulfilling what might have been expected of me had I gone the traditional route of college.

Which I didn't. My parents let me leave the house at 16 to go and live with Uncle Nick and Aunt Scotty in

Connecticut, because I had expressed a desire to get back into art in general and the art scene in New York City in particular. I think that my parents really wanted me to go to college, but they weren't the type to demand anything from me, preferring that I learn to make my own way in life.

"That's what you have always done, Dalilah," mom had said. "Always. So, far be it for me to stop you now. We want you to make your own decisions about your life, because you need to own what you do. Nobody else can own your life but you. Remember that."

That had made a lot of sense to me. They were basically saying that I needed to find my own path without their pushing me into anything. Alaina was jealous of this, of course. Her parents were forcing her to apply to every Ivy League college there was, which she did, being the ever dutiful daughter. Of course, she was really like a female Eddie Haskell, in that she was obsequious to a fault to the face of her elders, but, behind their backs, she was the wildest girl I had yet to know. And she was over 1200 miles away from her suffocating parents, who still lived in the Kansas City area, so she was pretty much into everything. Prescription drugs, alcohol, even some street stuff that I would never think about trying. I heard too many horror stories from my father to ever think about doing some of the things that Alaina was doing.

But alcohol? Oh, yeah. I was sucking that stuff down like water. Because I was still directionless. No matter how much I tried, I couldn't seem to get the muse back. So, I modeled for art classes, hoping against hope that these young students would inspire some kind of spark of creativity in me again. But they never did.

So, I pretty much did the nude modeling gigs to pay the bills and nothing more. The university gigs paid pretty low by New York City standards – only around $25 an hour. But the private gigs that I managed to score paid around $100 an hour, so I was able to maintain my financial independence from my parents, however tenuously, while I pretty much waited for my well-spring of creativity to activate in me once more.

In the meantime, I had my bottles of Cuervo and Jack, my random men, and Seth whenever I wanted him. These things kept me company. So did Alaina, who was not only experimenting with drugs but with her sexuality as well. She kissed me one drunken night at my apartment, and we ended up in bed together. It had happened three times since then, and it was…nice. I guess. About as good as Seth, really.

I changed into my robe and glared at Kyle. "What?"

"Missy, if you weren't so goddamned physically flawless, I would have canned your sweet ass a long time ago. Now get out there."

I rolled my eyes, and stepped out in front of the waiting class. They were buzzing restlessly. I saw quite a few canvasses with no students behind them, as the students in question obviously had gotten fed up and left. There was a guy sitting on the back table, tossing a ball in the air, while a girl sat at his feet, playing with her phone and grabbing onto his leg playfully. A few students were drawing and painting diligently, but, mainly, the students were in various stages of boredom and ennui.

I took off my robe and stood in front of the class. Immediately, the buzzing stopped, and the students' eyes were trained on me. I sighed a little bit in relief, and laid down on the blanket that was placed on the hard surface. Within two minutes, every student was behind their canvas, painting diligently.

I wanted to address the class and apologize for my lateness. It wasn't like me to be so disrespectful, but I had really drank to the point of blacking out the previous night, so getting up and making this 9 AM class was more than a challenge. Especially since I had to come from Queens. How I made it to Queens last night in my inebriated state was a mystery that I had not yet contemplated. I could only assume that Mystery Boy had called a cab for both of us to take from the Village bar that I was getting hammered in.

God, I hope there were condoms involved. I had no desire to end up back in the clinic to get another prescription for antibiotics or whatever it is that they give you when you end up with chlamydia. Yeah, virtually everyone I knew had that particular disease at least once, but it didn't make it any less embarrassing. And, god forbid I get something else that wasn't so curable. I had thus far been lucky that way, unlike Janelle, who hung out with Alaina and me. She was exposed to the herp, the gift that keeps on giving, and was constantly dealing with painful outbreaks that caused her to have to often miss class.

As I laid there, the students dispassionately staring at me, and then quickly tending to their canvases, I started to feel the familiar feeling of wanting to hurl. I really think that I was still drunk when I started this particular gig, and the alcohol had finally worked its way through my system, and all that I wanted right at that moment was some kind of bucket or something. I swallowed hard, and stared at the lights, hoping that they might distract me. I imagined that, since Kyle was already so pissed at me for being late, he probably would end up canning me if I would have puked all over the floor. And getting up and running to the bathroom was not an option. These students were in the flow, and my leaving right at that moment would have been more than unfair to them.

Damn, this is the longest half hour of my life. Thank god I was a half hour late, because I literally didn't think that I ever could have laid there for the full hour. I imagined that the students might have painted my face a bit green, then laughed to myself for thinking that.

Finally, the class was over, and the students started packing up their tools and canvases. They lingered around the classroom, talking to one another, trying hard not to look at me as I stood up and put on my white robe and slippers. I quickly ran back to the back room, as the urge to vomit once again presented itself, and I finally found relief in hovering over the toilet.

Kyle came over disapprovingly. "Not preggers, I hope. Aw, but, then again, that might be interesting. Give the kids a different kind of female form to draw."

I looked up at him. "No, not pregnant. I'm using something. Just a long night last night, that's all."

"How long?" he asked, his hands on his hips. Kyle could be such a queen sometimes.

"I left the strange Queens apartment at 8 this morning. Hence my being a half hour late. You know how long it takes to get here from Queens with all the transfers."

Kyle just shook his head. "Do your parents have any idea what you're doing? Aren't you supposed to, you know, be an art student instead of an art model?"

"No offense, Kyle, and I hope that this doesn't sound too arrogant. But I studied all the masters, starting when I was five years old. Between the age of 5 and 11, I was more prolific than almost any working artist you could name today. I had showings at the *Luhring* and the *Bonakdar*," I said, referencing two Chelsea galleries that worked with artistic powerhouses from around the globe. "So I really don't know what I could possibly learn in a classroom that hasn't already been self-taught."

Kyle narrowed his eyes. "You do know that I can Google what you just said, don't you, Dalilah Gallagher?"

I shrugged my shoulders. "Go right ahead. I'm not lying about that."

He looked skeptical and brought out his phone. After a minute or so, his eyes got wide in astonishment. "You really weren't kidding. My god, your work was so…"

"Mesmerizing and raw?" I said. "Heard it all before."

"You were how old when you got these showings?" he asked, as he flipped through the Google images of my work.

"I was 10 when I got my first major showing. I also got a showing at the *Magda Danysz* in Paris that same year."

"10. For the love of god, what have you been doing lately?"

I shrugged my shoulders. "I quit. I lost my voice and my inspiration. I found that I no longer had anything to say."

"Nothing to say? You mean to tell me that you were a has-been by the age of 11?"

"That's exactly what I'm telling you. But, art has always been the only thing that interests me, so I'm desperately trying to get it back. To find my voice again. It hasn't been easy. I thought that just being in the environment with fledgling artists, and especially being in the environment of the established ones for which I model, would inspire me to pick up my brush again. But I have found that I still go home and stare at an empty canvas night after night."

"Oh, I see. So, you go out to the bars and get shit-faced so that you don't have to sit home and stare at that canvas."

I put my finger on my nose and smiled. "You catch on quickly."

He shook his head. "Dalilah. Running from your problems isn't going to solve them."

"No, but getting shit-faced helps me forget about them for a least a short period of time. They're still there, as big as life, when I'm living in reality. But, for a few hours, as I sip my Tanqueray and tonic, my inadequacies seem less so. It's merciful, really."

"You know, you mentioned once that you left school at age 16 and moved here. Maybe that has something to do with it, too. Why you're wondering through life with all the direction of a feather in the wind."

"I'm sure that didn't help," I said, honestly. "But school wasn't doing me any good, either. It's very hard to concentrate in class when you're studying something that you've already mastered before the age of 7. Which would encompass most of the material in my high school courses. Even the advanced courses. I was about ready to jam my pencil into my brain, I was so bored."

"So," he said. "You've been in this city for three years then. And in that time, you've accomplished…."

"Let's not go into that, okay? I'd rather not have to contemplate it."

"You've answered my question," he said.

"I'm glad," I said. "Now, if you don't mind, I'm going to get dressed and get on the subway and go…somewhere." I didn't really know where I was going to go. Seth was working, of course, and Alaina was in class. Unfortunately, today was one of the days that I didn't have a private gig. On such days, I found myself wandering the city endlessly. More often than not, I got into trouble.

"Well, okay, then. But, little girl, tomorrow morning. 9 sharp. One more late day, and you'll find yourself on the street. Are we clear?"

"Crystal," I said.

I got dressed and went down to the street. I went up to a street vendor and grabbed a bagel and lox and sat down on a bench to eat it.

On the other bench was an extraordinarily handsome and well-dressed man. Despite the fact that it was 50 degrees, which meant that I was dressed in a cardigan, the man had on a trench coat. His black hair was slicked back, and his eyes were a cerulean blue. In spite of myself, I found myself staring at him. He looked so familiar….

I shook my head, and continued to eat my bagel. But I soon became aware that he was trying to catch my eye. I could see it in my peripheral vision. So, I looked up again.

Then it struck me. I had seen him before. Many times before, in fact. It never occurred to me that this guy seemed to be everywhere I went, for whatever reason. It just registered when I took a good look at his face.

I smiled, for he was staring at me. His stare was penetrating and cold, and it made me feel uncomfortable. He raised his cup of coffee to his lips and continued to stare.

Finally, he held out his hand for me to shake. "Blake," he said. "Blake Nottingham."

"Dalilah," I said, although I had the feeling that he already knew my name. Just a hunch, but I was rarely wrong about such things. "Dalilah Gallagher."

"Dalilah. So, what brings you to this bench in the middle of the day?"

I shrugged. "Don't really have a place to go, I guess. Except home. But that's just too depressing. What about you?"

He smiled a little. "I'm the boss. I set my own hours." It was then that he gave me one of his cards. *Blake Nottingham, CEO, Nottingham Industries*, the card read. I recognized the name of the company, for it was a large software developer, with its world headquarters in Lower Manhattan.

Eh, so he's a big wig. So what? So is my dad. But there was something in those eyes of his that were very much not like my father's. My dad's eyes were kind, humorous. Full of life and warmth. He never took himself all that seriously, and he had some serious passion for my mother, even after all these years. They kind of grossed me out when I lived there, because I knew that, unlike most of my friend's parents, mine did It. A lot.

But this guy….he looked demanding. Cruel, even.

I shifted uncomfortably in my bench, and brought my bagel to my lips again. I looked over, and he was still staring at me. Lustfully. That was the only way that I could have explained it. He looked like he wanted my lips to be someplace else, other than on that bagel.

Finally, I finished my bagel and looked over my shoulder and saw a bus approaching. "Well, it's really good to meet you, Blake," I said, gesturing to the bus. "But I have to go."

"But you said that you didn't have anywhere to go," Blake said, his eyes now registering hurt. "I was hoping to get to know you better."

Stalker. "Well," I said. "Sorry to disappoint. I'll uh, see you later." And the funny thing was, I knew that I was right about that.

Somehow I was going to run into him again. He wanted something from me, that was clear.

And I had a pretty good feeling on what that was.

Chapter Two

Luke

"Oh, mother fucker, not again." I had just arrived home, after putting in a double-shift at O'Leary's, which was the dive bar that was directly below my Brooklyn apartment. And, of course, I came home to find out that I had been robbed. Again. It was the third time in as many months.

Goddammit. I knew that I shouldn't have splurged and bought that big-screen television. I knew it when I bought it. *Luke* I had said to myself. *Now you know that you're only going to have this TV for a month at the most. So, don't get too attached.* Yeah, I didn't much want to get attached to it, but yet I did. I somehow imagined that this might be the year when I actually could have something halfway decent. But, no. This wasn't my year after all.

Thank god I bought the damned thing hot. Otherwise, I'd have to really hunt the bastards down and somehow get them on the subway platform and push them off. I rubbed my hands together gleefully at the thought, then felt badly for thinking this. These stupid thieves were probably trying to survive, just like me.

I didn't even bother to call the cops. What could they do? This shit was never recovered. It would end up in some pawn shop, and I would see it there when I would bring in some things that would serve as collateral for a loan, and then get pissed when I realized that I would have to buy my own shit back.

Same as the other two times I got shit stolen. The most frustrating thing in the world is to see my stuff on the wall of some pawn shop, and know that there was no way I could get it unless I paid for it again.

Ridiculous. Ridi-fucking-culous.

Grrrrr....there were days, like today, when I questioned my sanity for blindly following my dreams to this city. Those dreams were increasingly meeting a dead end. Which wasn't fucking fair. I was goddamned talented. I knew that I was. Yet I couldn't get a showing if I whored myself to do it. And, trust me, there were times when I thought about doing just that. Hell, I would even do gay-for-pay if it meant that I could get just one showing in this town.

But no. I had to make do with my measly tips at the bar, combined with the small sales that I would realize whenever I could get a booth at one of the local art fairs. I could never sell my paintings for much, of course, because I didn't have the name. But everybody always oohed and aahed over them, so I must have been doing something right.

Even my website was generating few hits. I was just about ready to call it quits and proclaim myself an abject failure. Go home to Portland, Maine and be a fisherman. It was good enough for my old man, so it really should be good enough for me.

Frustrated, I laid down on my couch, and stared at my

guitar. I picked up a Rubik's Cube that was on the coffee table, and twisted it, as I dreamed up some lyrics. My canvas was in the middle of the room, mocking me. I flipped it off, and continued to work the cube until I solved it. Which never took me very long. I had long since mastered that thing.

Then I brought out a bong, put some pot into the slide, lit it, sucked on it, and laid back down. I felt my blood pressure diffusing as I laid on my couch and looked at the ceiling. After a few more hits, I picked up my guitar and my sheet, where I was writing down notes for one of the many songs that I had jumbled in my head, waiting to be transcribed onto the paper. I strummed a few notes, and then wrote them down on the sheet. The musical part always came easily to me. The lyrics, not so much, but I was always working on it.

I took a few more hits, and, satisfied with the amount of work that I had put into my song-writing, I got up and sat down in front of my canvas. In a few minutes, I was picturing a girl that I had seen that day on the bus. She was a pretty girl, very pretty, with red hair and gorgeous sensuous lips. She had a contemptuous look on her beautiful face, like she wasn't having a good day. Like she perpetually wasn't having a good day. But there was something in her beautiful green eyes that made me look a second time, and then a third time. I found myself studying her from the time that she got on, until the time that she got off, which was about a half-hour later. I had looked out the window and saw her wandering into a bar in Uptown, and, if it weren't for the fact that I had to get to a meeting, where I hoped to get some commissioned work, I would have gotten off and followed.

But, it was just as well, as I had to be at my bartending

job that evening anyhow. It wouldn't be good to lose my only steady source of income, which might have happened if I didn't show up for my shift. Something told me that missing a shift because I wanted to follow a pretty girl into a bar probably wouldn't go over so well with my own bosses.

And, of course, the Uptown meeting went nowhere, as the meetings with these rich bastards often do. They loved my work. They would be in touch. Yeah, right. In touch. Whatever.

I sketched the girl's face with my pencil lightly, and then brought out my colored pencils and rapidly filled the rest of it in. In a half-hour, I had a good likeness of her face. I sat back and smiled, and felt the melting of the rest of the stress that I had felt when I came home and saw that my apartment was robbed.

It was really a masterpiece, I thought, so I decided to add it to my portfolio. I had yet another meeting the next day with yet another rich bastard, and maybe this sketch would help me get the job.

Chapter Three

I woke up with a start and glanced at my clock. I had fallen asleep on the couch the previous night, still dressed in my jeans and t-shirt. I had just a few too many hits, to be perfectly honest, which would be why I had forgotten to set my alarm.

Oh, fuck. I had forgotten to set my alarm! I frantically looked at the clock, and saw that it read 7 AM. 7 AM. My meeting with Nottingham Industries was set for 8. One hour. One hour to somehow make it from my Brooklyn apartment to the headquarters for Nottingham Industries in lower Manhattan.

I rushed off the couch, and looked in the mirror. My hair was pretty much askew and I had a definite 5 o'clock shadow. But it couldn't be helped. I had no time to shower or change or anything else. I had to get the bus, and then get the subway, and then somehow, someway, make it to the Nottingham headquarters. All in under an hour.

So, I picked up my portfolio, dashed out the door, and

then literally ran after the bus, as it was pulling off the stop right when I got on the street. I frantically ran it down, and it pulled over for me, thank god. That was unusual. Bus drivers don't usually do that. But this one did, so I would forever think of this bus driver, one James Mancini, according to his name tag, as being my savior. Forget Jesus. When had Jesus ever stopped a bus for me between stops?

My heart racing, I swiped my card. "Thanks so much," I said.

"Not a problem," said the bus driver, although I knew differently. It really was a problem for the bus to come to a stop right in the middle of the street.

I took my seat and put on my ear buds. I tried not to silently curse my own stupidity and lack of organization, but my mind kept returning to these very themes. Sometimes I amazed even myself with my endless capacity for self-destruction. I really needed to take this opportunity more seriously, along with any other opportunities that might crop up. After all, it could mean that I could eat something other than Kraft Macaroni and Cheese that month.

I guessed that I really didn't take it seriously because it probably would go nowhere. It was exceedingly difficult to get commissioned work. Almost as difficult as it was to get a decent showing. I was starting to realize one thing – and that was that the image of the starving artist wasn't as romantic and glamorous as it is portrayed to be. It really sucked donkey balls to be absolutely honest.

I finally got to the subway station, and hurriedly bought my pass and got on. I arrived at the Nottingham Headquarters with very little time to spare, but at least I wasn't late. I looked like crap, and I hadn't showered or shaved, but I was there. I suppose that was all that mattered.

I took the elevator to the 75th Floor of the gleaming building. I arrived at the suite and announced my name to the bored-looking receptionist. She nodded her head and got on her phone and indicated that I should take a seat. Which I did.

I inhaled deeply, and took in the unmistakable smell of jasmine. I supposed that this was meant to be relaxing. If so, it wasn't working, because I was just as anxious as ever.

Of course, they kept me waiting. Cooling my jets on their white leather couch. Rich bastards were all the same, really. They were just sooo important, too important to ever try to actually be on time. But god forbid you were even a few minutes late. God forbid. They held all the power, and they knew it.

Finally, after I kicked myself repeatedly for busting my ass to be there right on time, and thinking that I should have taken a few minutes to comb my hair and shower after all, the receptionist addressed me.

"Mr. Roberts," she said. "Mr. Nottingham will see you now."

I glanced at my watch. 8:45. Bastard was 45 minutes late. Well, okay, just as well. Let's get this over with.

The receptionist lady, who was wearing a too-tight pencil skirt and red cardigan sweater, combined with fuck-me pumps, led the way to the enormous conference room. At the end of the table was the rich bastard in question. Black slicked hair, cold blue eyes, impeccably dressed. I supposed that he was one of those guys who had his shoes shined to a glass-like sheen every morning. He had a personal tailor, no doubt, and he probably never, ever left the house without making sure that every hair was in place.

I self-consciously touched my own hair, wanting it to lay

down a little bit. I reached my hand over to the guy in an effort to shake his hand, but he literally waved me away.

Well, this meeting is starting off swimmingly. I sat down, and he gestured to me to give him my portfolio. I passed it to him, and he opened it up without a word.

I silently watched him flipping through the portfolio, his expression inscrutable. I could only assume that he was feeling somewhat less-than-impressed. To say the very least. I tapped my fingers on the table and stared out the window. Cursed what seemed to be yet another trip into the city for nothing. I could have just stayed home and strummed my guitar and finished the song that I was writing. Or got caught up on some badly-needed sleep. Or gotten baked, although I was really trying to cut back on that aspect of my life at least a little bit, as I didn't want to become a wake and baker like some of my buddies.

He rapidly went through most of my paintings and sketches, boredom evident in his eyes. But, then, he stopped. And stared. I cocked my head, trying to see what master-piece had caught his eye, but I couldn't see what it was. All that I knew was that he suddenly had stopped flipping rapidly through the pages and had settled upon something. His expression had changed from one of insouciance and ennui to one of actually being interested.

Finally, he shut the book and looked at me. "Mr. Roberts," he said, "I would like to commission a project for me."

I looked at him, startled. I wondered if I had heard him correctly. I tried to hide my inner excitement at this sudden change of fate. "Tell me about the project that you're inter-ested in."

He pointed to the page that he was apparently staring at earlier, and motioned me to look at the drawing to which he was referring. "This girl," he said. "You captured her beautifully. Her very essence. Her sensuality. Her vulnerability. Her radiance. I want you to paint her nude. I'll pay you $10,000 to do so."

Whoa. Whoa. Whoa. $10,000? Was I hearing him correctly? And just because I happened to sketch the beautiful red-head on the bus? I pretended to be cool about it, though, even though my insides were doing cartwheels. So, I shrugged my shoulders. "That's a little bit below my going rate." That was bullshit, of course. My going rate was pretty much whatever they would be willing to pay me. This guy could tell me that he would pay me $50 to paint her, and I would have taken that job. I was kinda a whore that way.

He shut the book. "Okay, then, Mr. Roberts, I'll find somebody else to complete this project."

Oops. I overplayed my hand in my utter excitement, which was caused by my finally getting a bite. "Well, I'll make the exception for you, of course."

He raised an eyebrow and stared at me. Just….stared. He put one of his fingers up to his cheek and continued to stare at me. I had to admit that I was feeling pretty intimidated right about then, but I managed to stare at him right back. No way did I want him to see what was really going on underneath the surface. *Please, oh please, let me do this project. I was a dumb-ass for trying to shake you down for more, but, come on, you seemed so anxious to get this project up off the ground, so I just thought that you would pay any amount. God knows you can afford it.*

I realized that I was holding my breath, and that he was still wordlessly staring at me. Finally, he pushed the book over to me. "Okay. My secretary will send over a contract. You can start tomorrow."

I felt like pumping my fist in the air. *Oh my god. I'm going to make more money off of this one project than I made all last year on my art. I might even be able to quit the bar, although that was unlikely. One project does not a career make.* I had to remind myself of this.

"Cool," I said. "Are you going to contact the subject, or should I?"

"I will," he said. "I'll send her over to your art studio in the morning. You do have an art studio?"

I nodded my head. Of course I did. Such as it was. It really was an abandoned warehouse where I believe that I had obtained squatting rights. I really never used it, though, as I couldn't ever afford to actually hire models to paint. Until now, that is. Really, I should have taken some of that $10,000 and invested in a better studio to paint this woman, but there wasn't time to do all that before the project would have begun. And, it didn't seem that any of that money would be provided to me in advance. I didn't ask, but I would imagine that to be the case. So, she was just going to have to meet me in the abandoned warehouse. Thank god I was able to actually supply a generator so that there was some kind of electricity flowing through.

He was staring at me again. Really, he was a fucking weirdo, the way that he was staring all the time. But I soon realized that he wanted information, and that staring was his way of conveying this. Lucky me, I caught on quickly.

"Oh, you want the address to my studio, don't you?" I asked him.

"Yes. Please supply this."

"Okay," I said, feeling foolishly underprepared. "Could you get your secretary in here to write it down? I forgot to bring a pen and paper."

He sighed, and pushed his finger on the button of the

phone. "Amelia, could you please come in here. And bring a pen and paper."

He hung up and stared at me some more. This time, I didn't try to stare back. I was sick and tired of him intimidating me in such a way.

Amelia appeared at the door, pen and paper in hand. Blake said nothing to her, but, rather, communicated with a silent gesture in my direction. She understood, for she approached me and gave me the materials that she had brought in. "Here, Mr. Roberts," she said.

"Thanks," I said, and then scribbled the address on there. She gave him the piece of paper, and he nodded.

"I will send Ms. Gallagher this address with instructions to meet you tomorrow morning at 8," he said.

"Cool," I said.

"Do not be late," he warned me. "She'll see you tomorrow morning."

"Okay," I said, rising from my chair. "Well, peace out. I guess I'll be seeing Ms. Gallagher tomorrow. By the way, what is her first name?"

He narrowed his eyes at me. "Dalilah. I have to confess that I'm surprised that you don't know this."

"Well, I mean, I don't know her. I just happened to be behind her on the bus yesterday. She stuck out in my mind."

He blinked his eyes and said nothing.

"Okay, well, then, I guess that I'll be going," I said. "Uh, thanks for this opportunity."

He nodded and said nothing. And then he put his head down and started writing something. Something that I would imagine was completely unrelated to what we had just spoken about. I shrugged my shoulders and went out the door.

I couldn't stop smiling, though, as I got the elevator and rode it down to the ground floor. I couldn't believe my good fortune in getting this commission. It was crazy how much I couldn't believe that I had lucked into this job.

I couldn't wait to get started.

Chapter Four

Dalilah

The bartender came around, wiping the bar area in front of me. He noticed that I was dry. "You need another one, Dalilah?"

I looked at my now empty glass, and brought it to my lips. I crunched on the ice, and pushed the glass to him. "Sure, bring it on," I said. I looked at my watch, thinking that I was going to have to blow off Seth again. Why he put up with my crap, I really didn't know. It was so obvious to myself that I really didn't care about him, any more than I did in high school, when he was all about getting me to go out with him just once. Sometimes I wondered why I had even started dating him, if you could call it that. It was just something that I had fallen into when I just happened to run into him when I was at the Met one day.

Looking back, I realized that it was a particularly lonely time for me. I had just moved out of Nick and Scotty's home, which they allowed me to do when I turned 18, and

Alaina was not yet in the city. She hadn't started school at that time. So, I kinda knew nobody, and running into Seth was somewhat comforting. He and I ended up having lunch, and then ended up in bed about two hours later, and it was all very…nice. That was really all that I could say about that. It was nice. After all, he really was a handsome guy, with his full lips, hazel eyes, long dark eyelashes, thick dark hair and rock-hard body. He was the kind who made every girl swoon, always. Every girl but myself.

Of course, it meant much more to him than it did to me. He told me as much as I laid around in his bed that day, not really wanting to return back to my empty apartment. "I knew that you would come around, Dalilah," he had said. "I thought it would have happened a lot sooner than this, though."

I said nothing, not really wanting to tell him that I hadn't, in fact, come around. I didn't want to burst his bubble. Which was probably much of the reason why I continued to see him. That, and the fact that he sometimes supplied me with groceries when I got low. I never could hide my ennui, though, with him, and I felt a little bit badly because of this.

I went outside the bar, nodding to Tom, the bartender, "watch my drink for me, okay?" I said. "I have to make a phone call."

"Sure thing," he said. "Hurry back."

I got outside the building, and dialed Seth's number. He picked up on the second ring. "Dalilah," he said.

"Hi," I said. "Hey, I need a rain check for tonight."

He was silent on the other end. "Okay. Whatever." He was obviously annoyed, for he didn't bother to ask me why I needed said rain check.

"Yes," I said. "Well, I guess I'll be seeing you."

"I wouldn't count on it."

"Okay," I said, simply. Then I hung up the phone. I couldn't be bothered to care about poor Seth. All I knew was that there was a glass of whiskey that was waiting for me at the bar.

I got home that night and was greeted by a most unpleasant surprise, considering my inebriated state. My father was sitting in my living room, waiting for me to come home.

Oh, crap. He was the last person that I wanted to see right at that moment. He had his arms crossed. He obviously wasn't pleased with me.

"Dad," I said. He was blurry, not in focus. My stomach started rumbling, and I, once again, had to stop myself from vomiting.

"Dalilah," he said, his voice stern. "You need to have a seat."

It suddenly occurred to me that perhaps there was something wrong. Maybe something had happened to my mom. But, no, it wasn't that, because my mom soon appeared in the living room as well. She, too, looked like she wanted to kick my ass.

"Mom," I said, my heart sinking. This wasn't looking good. "How are you?"

"Dalilah Rose Gallagher," she said, and I knew I was in serious trouble. Whenever mom used all three of my names, it meant that shit was about to go down. "You-"

My dad made a motion for her to be quiet. Then he turned to look at me. "Dalilah," he said. "We've been hearing disturbing reports about your lifestyle out here."

"Reports?" I said, feeling a bit panicked. "From who?"

"Nick," he said.

"Nick. How the hell does he know anything about my lifestyle? I haven't been living with him for two years now."

He was quiet. Then it occurred to me that Nick probably had some kind of plant in the bar that I frequented. It would be just like my dad and Nick to be sneaky like that. God knew that they both were involved in any number of sneaky things over the years. Not to mention the fact that my father was a serious drug addict when he was my age. As far as I was concerned, he, especially, had zero moral authority to tell me anything. Nick, too. Before he met Scotty, he slept around way more than I could have ever dreamed of doing.

Finally, he spoke. "Listen. Your mom and I agreed to let you come out here because we both wanted you to be immersed in the art culture. Art is your passion, and it always has been. That was the main reason why we agreed not to push you to go to college. Well, that and the fact that nobody has ever been able to push you into anything that you don't want to do. Which is besides the point. But Nick has gotten a report that you have been spotted getting drunk at a bar here in town several times, and that you have left with a stranger each of those times."

"Oh my god. And what are you going to do? I'm a legal adult. You can't very well force me to come home with you while I straighten out and learn to fly right."

"No," he agreed. "I can't. But Dalilah, I want you to know that your mom and I have decided that we need to be closer to you. So, I just purchased a house in the Montauk. That will be our new home base."

Montauk? Of course, my dad would choose to live in the Hamptons. God forbid he would live among the

26

unwashed. "Montauk. And what about *Dalilah's Friends*? What about your foundation?"

"*Dalilah's Friends* is in excellent hands. I'm going to do something similar here. I'm going to start a new sanctuary just outside of town. Which is why I am choosing to live in Montauk. That will be closer to where my new sanctuary will be. As for the foundation, I'm much closer to power brokers in New York City than in Kansas City."

In my drunken state, my feelings were a bit dulled, but the horror was there, all the same. Suddenly, I had to deal with my parents being a little over two hours away. "Okay, so you're virtually moving into this city. And this will change my life how?"

Finally, my mother spoke. "Dalilah. We would like for you to have dinner with us at least once a month. I feel like we've been shut out of your life. You never answer the phone when we call. God forbid you would ever call us back. You don't even answer the phone when Nick calls. I don't approve of you doing what you're doing. You're wasting – "

"My potential. I know. God, don't I know. Trust me, as disappointed as you are in me, I'm about 1000 times more disappointed in myself. You think that I like myself this way? Do you think that I want to stare at an empty canvas night after night? You have no idea what it's like to be an artist. To want to eat, drink and breathe creativity and art. But realizing that there really is no air. There's no air because you're suffocating. I can't breathe art, because I can't get past my mental blocks."

My father shook his head. "What happened to you, Dalilah? What happened to the fearless little girl who created some of the leading urban expressionistic paintings and sculptures in the world?"

I just stared at him, and then simply said "I guess I'm not fearless anymore. I can't silence my inner critic, so I'm…paralyzed."

I looked down at the floor. My dad understood. I knew that he did. He, too, was an artist, and an amazing one at that. But he never went anywhere with it, even though he had some early success, for basically the same reason I quit. And that is the haters. The haters who exist to tear people down. They might be jealous or they might have mental issues. They might merely be trolls. But for somebody with an artistic temperament, they can be devastating to creativity. So, my dad mainly painted for himself and my mother. And he ended up working for The Man. With all of his absolute genius and artistic prodigiousness, he still ended up working as a soulless bank president for many years, before he finally found his passion in working with animals.

Again, my father had zero authority to talk to me about anything. He gave up his own dreams of being an artist. He had a serious drug addiction when he was my age. Everything that he would be saying to me would ring hollow. It would be a case of "do as I say, not as I do." And if there was one thing that I couldn't stand, it was a fucking hypocrite.

As for my mother. Well, I guess she had a little bit more authority to advise me than my father. She had managed to avoid serious substance abuse, except for those two weeks after she was raped all those years ago. But her hands weren't clean, either. She was a goddamned cutter at my age. As for her career, she pretty much rode the coattails of my father. If it weren't for him, she would be some kind of two-bit lawyer just scraping by, because that was what she was when she met my dad.

I looked at them, well aware of my defensive posture. If

I could read their minds, I would imagine that they were either regretting the fact that they both were such fuck-ups when they were my age, or they were regretting telling me exactly how much they were fuck-ups. They sat me down when I was very young and told me all about their idiot mistakes, mainly because it was all chronicled in a *People* magazine, and they figured that I would come across it sooner or later. My mom's drug addiction wasn't in that magazine, though, as it happened later. So her telling me about that was a bonus, I guess.

"Dalilah," my father said. "You have to get over it. You have to set aside your fear of failure and realize that you have a gift. You have an amazing gift, no matter what that goddamned Henry Jacobs might have said."

Henry Jacobs. Just hearing that name made my blood pressure shoot. He was the one who destroyed me. And, what's more, I still believe that it was his intention to do so. He didn't do an honest review of my work. There was no way that what he wrote could have ever been considered to be honest. It was motivated by his daughter, who was pedestrian at best and couldn't stand the fact that I was only 11 and was already attaining international acclaim. My Parisian showing at the *Magda Danysz*, which is one of the most renowned galleries in the world, was the final straw for the little witch.

But Henry Jacobs was like a Pied Piper. He was one of the most renowned critics on the *New York Times*, and when he wrote something, the sycophants usually followed. Suddenly, they started writing stories about how the Emperor really had no clothes. Me being the Emperor in this analogy. Before that goddamned *New York Times* review of my showing at *Luhring*, I was widely becoming known as the "Mozart of the art world." Just as Mozart was composing music at the age of five, I began painting seriously at that same age. Early critics also stated that my work would be influential on the art world, much as Mozart's music had been profoundly influential on the music world. I was hailed as a fearless pioneer, who was blazing a trail with my subject matter and my technique. Of course, any comparison to Mozart would have been overblown at best. Nobody would ever be able to compare to him, in any kind of artistic endeavor. The comparison was mainly drawn because I was such a prodigy.

After Henry Jacobs, though, it all went to hell. Suddenly, the critics decided that my work was stale and lifeless. Prosaic and derivative. It was as if these other critics really took their cues from Jacobs the big dog, and if Jacobs decided that I was a fraud, then that became the conventional wisdom.

It was the first time that I had started having doubts about myself. I really was fearless before that Jacobs article. I took chances that other artists didn't. I decided that I would turn the genre of urban expressionism on its head. That was what I was aiming for, and I felt unstoppable. But the cascades of poor reviews that happened after the Jacobs article made me want to crawl into a hole and die. And the word "fearless" was no longer a part of my vocabulary, and it was never again used to describe my work.

I still tried to paint, but I started to look at my own work as being stale and derivative. Prosaic and lifeless. And I would rip up every painting I attempted during this time. I hated every one of them. I believed the critics completely, and decided that I really didn't have anything meaningful to say. I was still an artist, through and through. It was still the only thing that I had ever wanted. But I couldn't do it anymore.

I finally just sighed, as my father continued to stare at me, his eyes sympathetic. My mother still looked pissed, I guess because she really couldn't relate to me on the artistic level, unlike my dad. As far as she was concerned, I was an impetuous little brat who had won the genetic lottery and still became a waste. That was pretty unforgivable to her, I would imagine. My dad could also relate to my being an intellectual prodigy, because he was, too. He knew that it wasn't easy for me to truly fit into a world that was clearly stupid in so many ways. He understood how frustrating it was to be able to outthink 99.99% of the population on just about every issue.

So, I decided to give in a little. If only to try to please my father. My mother would never understand me, as much as she had always tried. But my father was a different story, so I wanted to try to please him.

"Okay, I'll have dinner with you every month," I said, conveniently ignoring my father's earlier plea for me to once again realize my gift and try to get over Henry Jacobs.

My mom looked happy. "That would be wonderful, Dalilah. That's all that we ask. We can keep up on your life so much better if we can have regular contact with you face to face."

My dad put his hand on my shoulder, and brought me to him in a big hug. To my surprise, I found myself crying as I listened to his heart beating. He stroked my hair and said "shhhhhh, Dalilah, you're okay. You're going to find your way, baby girl. Your mom and I love you very much. And we always believe in you. Always."

I nodded my head and said nothing.

But the tears kept coming, and it felt like they would never stop.

Chapter Five

I woke to my phone buzzing incessantly. It was then that I realized that I had turned off my phone after my Seth brush-off, not wanting to deal with the reality that he would be blowing up the phone, as he always did when I blew him off. I had turned the phone back on after I went to bed at 4 AM. I had stayed up with my parents, talking late into the night about everything under the sun. My father was still trying to reach me in his way. My mom, too, but she tended to go about it in a manner that pushed me further away as opposed to bringing me closer.

They had already left, as they had a hotel room, because they knew that there was no way that they could stay with me in my studio apartment.

Now, here it was 7 AM, and my phone was ringing. I was in no mood to talk to anyone, as I was once again hungover and talking with my parents had emotionally drained me. But I picked up anyhow.

"Dalilah Gallagher," said a familiar voice on the other end. "I have been trying to get ahold of you. Why haven't you been picking up your phone and returning your messages?"

I was incredulous. Whoever was speaking was a pushy little bastard, and I didn't like it one bit. "Who is this?" I asked.

"This is Blake Nottingham. You met me a few days ago. I need you to pose, and I need this in one hour."

Blake Nottingham. The creeper from the sidewalk bench. Fuck that, I wasn't going to pose for him or anybody else in an hour. "Mr. Nottingham, I'm very sorry, but this is short notice. I'll have to take a rain check."

"You will not take a rain check. I have already arranged for the artist to meet you at 12667 Roosevelt Avenue in Queens."

I recognized that address, and I suddenly knew that there was no fucking way I would ever go down there. It was in the industrial area of Queens, known as Willets Point, and it was a cesspool. There was little there but junk-yards and waste processing plants. And abandoned ware-houses. Somehow, I got the feeling that 12667 Roosevelt Avenue would probably fall into that category.

I laughed. "I'm so sorry, Mr. Nottingham, but posing there is out of the question. I generally don't leave Manhattan for a job, and I certainly am not going to go to an armpit like Willets Point for anybody."

"I'll pay you $1,000," he said.

My eyebrows raised. Suddenly, I was interested. I could use that money, because I realized that Seth probably was going to cut me off, and there was just no way that I was going to go to my parents, hat in hand. That would be the nail in my coffin, having to beg for their financial support.

"I'll be there at 8," I said.

"Thank you," he said, and hung up.

I didn't have time to think about how this man got my personal phone number. I mean, a lot of established artists had my phone number, because I had been making the rounds and I had become somewhat in demand. But how this Nottingham person managed to get my phone number was beyond me.

I didn't have time to think about that one, though. I had to rush to get the bus and the right subway, and then more bus transfers to this little hell-hole in Queens.

Chapter Six

Luke

I actually did end up at my "studio" a little bit early, as I didn't want a repeat performance of the other morning. So, I didn't get baked the night before and actually got some sleep for once in my life. I knew that getting to the studio would be tricky on the bus, because I was going to have to carry my tools and my canvas on there. I really should have outfitted the studio with what I needed, but I used the place so little that there was never a point in doing that.

So, I packed up my stuff and took off on the bus to the Willets Point district of Queens. This was a depressing area that resembled a war zone, really, and I felt a little bad that a classy woman, as this Dalilah Gallagher seemed to be, would have to be subjected to such an indignity as coming to an abandoned warehouse in the middle of a post-apocalyptic landscape like Willets Point. But, it couldn't be helped. It was either here in this studio or in my studio apartment. And I had finally resorted to having bars installed on my windows, and the guys were coming today to install them, so painting this Dalilah in my apartment was out of the question. I never thought that I would have to resort to having bars on my windows, but being constantly robbed was getting old indeed.

My heart was pounding as I got to my warehouse and set up shop. I started the generator, which powered the lights and a space heater, which was necessitated by the fact that it was always cold in this place, for some odd reason. I set up my canvas and carefully inventoried my tools. I had gotten the contract that was sent over by courier, and it specified that I was to paint a nude portrait of her that was to be delivered in three months. The payment would be contingent upon the buyer being satisfied with the work, which would mean that I wouldn't be paid until the end of the project. Until then, I guess, I would live on Spaghetti-O's and Ramen Noodles, as usual.

There was even an addendum that specified that, if the buyer was satisfied with the work, I could exercise an extra $10,000 option to sculpt her. He would supply the marble. That was more than exciting to me. I was an excellent painter, but an even better sculptor. I just never really got the chance to sculpt, as I couldn't afford the materials. If I chose to exercise that addendum, I could take up to six months to deliver it.

I set up the pedestal for her to pose on. I was given rather detailed instructions on the pose that she was supposed to assume in this first session. I was also sent a fainting couch for her to lay on. The couch was royal red, and very traditional. I would assume that he wanted the final product to be in keeping with the look of the couch, which would mean that I would paint her in more of a classical style, as opposed to attempting something more *avant-garde*.

This guy seemed to be a micro-manager and a control freak, but, no matter, I was going to do what he said. Far be it for me to breach the contract in any way, which would mean that I wouldn't be paid the amount that we agreed to. I had a working knowledge of contract 101, and realized that the terms were not absolute. It depended upon my following the instructions that I had agreed to, to the letter.

I finally got everything set up and ready to go. I looked at my watch. It read 7:55. Dalilah was supposed to arrive around 8. I tapped my toe nervously, hoping that she would show. I needed the income, for sure, but, truth be told, I also was looking forward to seeing her. From the short time that I saw her on the bus, I could tell that she was radiant. Incandescent. She just exuded a certain kind of sensuality that emitted from her very presence. It was difficult to describe. All that I knew was that I was drawn to her, as if I was being pulled in by a tractor beam.

It occurred to me that my benefactor had obviously felt the same way about her, which would be why he was so eager for me to take this project. In which case, I probably shouldn't bite the hand that fed me, which was what I would have been doing if I started a love affair with her. But, then, I immediately put that thought out of my head, because a girl like that was out of my league anyhow. I was obviously going to have to make do with fantasizing about being with her. And there wasn't any way that I was going to not fantasize about being with her.

At the same time, I had to be professional. That was going to be exceedingly difficult, considering the circumstances, but I was going to have to look at her as just another model. I had painted many nudes over the course of my career, both when I was a student and a few times as a professional, whenever I had been able to score commissioned work before. I typically couldn't afford to hire them on my own, but there had been a few commissioned projects that featured nude models, and I never had an issue being a consummate professional with them.

The minutes ticked by slowly. I kept checking my watch, and started to feel the anxiety build. What if she couldn't make it? Wouldn't Nottingham call me and let me know about that? I started to feel just a bit foolish, coming down here and setting everything up. If she didn't show, I would just be the chump.

The anxiety built, as the time got to be 8:30, and then 8:45. I kept checking my phone, too, to see if Nottingham had contacted me, but there was never a message or a voice-mail from him. I tapped my foot impatiently, and started to feel let down by the whole thing. *I probably shouldn't have gotten my hopes up.*

Finally, around 9, there was a knock on my door. I took a quick peek in the mirror before I went to let her in. My hair was behaving, and I was dressed as professionally as I could be, as I had chosen a yellow sweater with a white button-down, jeans and oxford shoes. I had even bothered to spray some cologne and used after-shave. All in all, I felt at least a bit presentable.

My heart pounding, I opened the door. She was standing on the other side of the door, wearing jeans, a longish cashmere sweater and boots. Her gorgeous red hair was tied up behind her head, and she wasn't wearing any makeup. But even in her casual attire, with her unadorned face, she still glowed from within. The same heat that I felt from her as I admired her on the bus was still burning, white hot. It was something that I could feel, especially since she was so close, and she actually was going to interact with me.

She smiled, her teeth perfect. I had a hard time taking my eyes off of her lips. Her perfect, full, sensuous lips. I self-consciously licked my own lips as I fixated on hers. She held out her slender hand, her nails perfectly lacquered in a dark blue color that was almost black. "Hi," she said. "I'm Dalilah. And you must be Luke."

I took a deep breath, determined that I was going to be cool. "Yeah, Luke," I simply said, shaking her hand. I willed my hand not to tremble, which would belie my outer attempts to be casual. To my delight, my handshake with her was steadfast and unwavering.

She just kind of stood there, after I shook her hand, and looked around. "Well, I guess I have to disrobe for you. Where can I do that?"

I pointed wordlessly to the divider that I had set up in the middle of the room. She nodded and went behind it. I could hear her back there, humming a tune that I didn't quite recognize. Her singing voice was melodic and sweet. It seemed higher-pitched than her speaking voice, which was low, throaty and sexy as hell. Her speaking voice fit her image, which was that of a classy lady who exuded intelligence and breeding. As Fitzgerald might have observed, her voice was full of money. Which made her even more out of my league, it that was even possible.

I gasped a little, trying to cover that up as well, when she emerged from behind the divider. She was completely nude, of course, and her body was sheer perfection. Creamy white skin. Perfectly round breasts. Tapered waist and gorgeous, well-toned legs. I tried very hard not to stare, and had to remind myself, over and over again, that I was a professional and she was just another model. Just another job to do. As difficult as that was to do, considering the fact that Dalilah was as physically perfect as anybody I had ever seen, let alone painted, I simply had to suck it up and pretend that she was like one of the zaftig women that I usually ended up portraying.

"Where do you want me?" she asked, obviously not shy or demure. Of course, this was just another job for her too. I had to remind myself of that fact.

I pointed to the fainting couch. "Right there would be cool," I said.

"Oh, how nice. A fainting couch. I've always wanted to pose in one of these. So much nicer than the usual chair or hard surface." At that, she laid down on the couch, and assumed a rather provocative pose. She had a long tendril of flaming-red hair draped over one of her breasts, and she cocked her head ever so slightly. "How is this?" she asked.

I suppressed a smile and said nothing. And then I got behind my canvas, and started to lightly sketch her outline. I would fill in with broad brush-strokes after I composed her basic form. That would be the easy part. More difficult would be the minute details. That is the part that would take months. And, to really get to her essence, which was important if the portrait was to accurately portray her, I would have to get to know her. Her passions, her thoughts, her feelings, her sense of humor. That would come with time, of course. For now, for this session, I wanted to get a quick assessment of her form, which would come from my sketching her and also shooting her with my camera.

She saw my camera, which was sitting on a table next to me. "Are you going to shoot me, too?"

"Yeah," I said. "I try to get a quick sketching down first, though. I know, it seems ass-backwards, but that's how I roll."

"I know that I should have asked this of Nottingham when he called me this morning," she said. "But I might assume that this is going to be an on-going project. How long will I have to be here, and for how many hours a day?"

"I would say around two hours a day, and the project is due in three months. I hope that isn't a problem."

"Not at all," she said. "But, of course, I'm going to have to renegotiate my fee with Nottingham. He's only paying me for today, I presume. But, then again, perhaps I am being presumptuous. At any rate, that isn't your concern. Carry on."

I smiled, and then started to concentrate on getting her form exactly correct. I had little self-doubt when it came to my artistic abilities. I knew that I was good. That was why it was so frustrating for me to have to struggle so much, while lesser talents managed to win commissions and showings. To think that I was thisclose to becoming a street artist. Not that being a street artist was necessarily a bad thing, but it was beneath me.

I sketched and brush stroked her broad form for about two hours, and I could tell that she was becoming a little bit uncomfortable. I expected that. Frankly, I couldn't imagine having to lie still for hours on end. I think that I would get antsy after having to lie in the same position for a half hour.

"You look like you could use a break," I said. "I'm sorry that I didn't offer you this earlier, but would you like a bottled water?"

"I'm dying for one," she said.

I went to the little fridge that I had for my bottled waters and pops. It was a mini-fridge, like one would have in a dorm room. I got a bottled water out and gave it to her. She sucked it down in record time and asked for another one.

"Looks like you're thirsty," I observed, stating the obvious.

"Dehydrated, actually," she said, but didn't elaborate on why she was dehydrated. "How much longer do you think you might need me?"

"About an hour more. When can you come back?" I hoped that I didn't say that in an *I really want you to come back because I'm dying to get to know you better* way. In other words, I hoped that my tone did not belie my extreme eagerness to see her again, under any pretense possible.

"I'll have to check my calendar and get back with you," she said. "Let me get your card. I assume that your email address is on there?"

"You assume correctly."

"Good. I'm ready to pose some more, if you're ready."

"Good to go," I said, and sat down and painted some more. I wouldn't start on the details until later. As I said, I had to get to know her, in order for her essence to imbue the work.

After about an hour, I stretched and let her know that I was done with my sketching and painting, so I needed to take some photographs of her.

I took about fifteen photographs in rapid fashion, and let her know that she could get dressed and leave if she would like.

"Thanks," she said. "I'll just get dressed and show myself out."

"Okay," I said, feeling like a jerk that I wasn't going to be able to show her out myself. But I had to get everything packed up, and I didn't want to keep her. She seemed rather eager to be on her way, and I assumed that she had something important to do. She appeared to be somebody who generally had important things on her agenda.

She got dressed and then came out from behind the dividers. "Well, it was good to meet you," she said, holding out her delicate hand again.

I shook her hand and nodded. Felt like a jerk again. Truth be told, she might have thought me laconic, but I really was tongue-tied. I had never been around a woman who captivated me quite this much. I just hoped that she didn't think that I was some kind of a quiet loser type.

She smiled and opened the door and disappeared through it.

And I sat down on the couch and put my head in my hands. I was finally able to acknowledge my pounding heart and butterflies that were dancing around my insides. I was going to have to pull it together if this project was going to be successful.

Pulling it together was going to be more difficult than I had originally thought.

Chapter Seven

Dalilah

Well, that was interesting. Luke was not quite what I was expecting. I mean, I didn't really know exactly what I was expecting, but I guess that I wasn't imagining a guy who would be so…young. He wasn't much older than me. And he was really a cute guy. Loved the dimples, and the hair that didn't quite behave. He tried hard to make it all lay down, but he still had a few tufts here and there that went every which way. Which was kind of adorable, really. He was tall and lean and had eyes that weren't quite blue, or green, or hazel, but a combination of all three. Depending on how the light hit, they would change color, so I wasn't quite sure how to describe them. Except to say that they were beautiful.

But I wasn't quite sure how to take him. He was so quiet. I knew that was partially because he was concentrating, and he was a consummate professional. That was plain, even though his studio left much to be desired. Not that it was uncomfortable accommodations, but it was apparent that he was a squatter. The fainting couch was a nice touch, though. I wondered if he got that for himself, or Nottingham had sent it over. It seemed so out of place in the grungy surroundings. Like a Victorian lady in the middle of squalor.

I found myself feeling eager about actually seeing him again, which was unusual for me. I didn't feel excited about much anymore, it seemed. My senses had been so dulled for so long that the feeling of anything other than utter boredom was an alien one for me. Still, the feeling was still nascent, undefined. It wasn't quite enough to make me feel excited and alive just yet.

Excited and alive...those were two words that I hadn't used, in my head, to describe myself since I was young and idealistic and composing my cutting-edge art. I used to get the feeling that I couldn't wait to get to my canvas, because there were so many ideas that were in my head, I just had to get them out. I was so prolific, I could complete three paint-ings in the span of a few weeks, sometimes days. I wanted to tackle different mediums, including sculpture. I also wanted to try some fusion, blending urban expressionism with some of the more traditional genres. I was so creative then that I felt like I had heightened senses. Everything around me was magnified, and I drew my inspiration from the most banal things.

I used my art as my voice, to show my sensibilities to the world. To make commentary about the injustices that I perceived, and about some of the dichotomies that were inherent in our society, yet were constantly ignored. I juxta-posed images that were related to poverty, and blended them with images that were representative of wealth. Images of living our comfortable existence, blended with the images of what made us comfortable – including slave labor and animals suffering. That sort of thing. I wanted to be provocative and make people think. That motivated me even more than the very feeling of putting the paint on the canvas, which was a high in and of itself.

Then, once the artistic inspiration ran dry, so did my very essence. I was really repressed. Perhaps I was even depressed. I didn't really know. All that I knew was that I was on rote, and had been for a long, long time. For longer than I cared to remember.

Unfortunately, that kernel of a feeling didn't last too long. I got home, and sat down in front of my canvas, hoping that something would spring forth. When nothing did, I got up in frustration, and did what was familiar for me by then.

I went to my usual watering hole.

Chapter Eight

I was on my fourth drink of the night, when I turned around and saw him. Nottingham. He was there in the bar, looking over at me with interest. There wasn't a hair out of place, as usual, and he was perfectly clean-shaven. As usual. There was none of the casual insouciance of Luke in this man. He was very buttoned-up, and I could just tell that he was afraid of how others would perceive him. Unlike Luke, who dressed in tattered jeans and couldn't control his hair, nor did he seem to want to.

I looked away, not wanting to engage him in conversation, but he was soon sitting next to me anyhow.

"Dalilah," he said. "Fancy meeting you here."

"Yeah. Fancy," I said, calling bullshit in my head. The guy was a stalker. That was all there was to it.

"How did it go today?"

"Fine. I have to email Luke later on and find out when he wants me again. In fact, I think I'll do just that." At that, I brought out my phone and prepared to text Luke. But Nottingham took the phone away from me.

"Text him later. I really would like your full attention."

I raised an eyebrow, and put my hand out, palms up, wordlessly.

He just shook his head. "You'll get this later, when you've earned it, Dalilah."

Earned it? He did not just say that.

Still, I just let it slide. There wasn't a point in getting upset about it. I was never one to be tied to my phone, anyhow.

"Whatever. Okay, you have my attention. What would like to say to me?"

He took a sip of his drink, which appeared to be some kind of whiskey, and peered at me with those cold blue eyes of his. They weren't full of life like Luke's were. Or my father's. Or even my mother's. There was clearly something wrong with him.

"Dalilah," he said. "I'm rather taken with you. I'd like to see you on a more private basis."

"Thanks, Mr. Nottingham, but, if it's all the same to you, I'd rather keep things between us professional. And I'm having a difficult time remembering how you first came to see me. I mean, you've obviously been following me, or something of the sort. But how you first encountered me... I'm sorry, but that escapes me."

He looked quite hurt. "There was a party in the Hamptons. You were living with Nick O'Hara and his wife, Scotty. You were wearing a white sundress and sandals. I had never seen such a magnificent beauty in my entire life. I asked around the party about you, as casually as I could, as you were not yet 18 at the time. I was able to find out enough about you that I was able to...."

"Follow me," I said, perplexed. And it didn't take a rocket scientist to now know exactly how Nick found out about me and my drunken escapades and the random men that followed. My guess was that this weirdo had been in these bars all along, and I just didn't notice him before because I hadn't yet met him.

He said nothing, but took another sip of his drink. Thus confirming that he was, in fact, following me.

"So," I said. "How do you know Nick and Scotty?"

"My company does business with his firm. O'Hara, White and Stroker has been my company's architectural firm for years."

"I see. And you're on a first name basis with Nick, I gather?"

"I am."

"And you have been reporting to Nick that I've not exactly been living a pristine life out here."

"Well, my dear, it doesn't suit you to leave with men you don't know, after you have been over-served. I think that you know this. I was only trying to look out for your best interests."

"My best interests will be determined by me. And nobody else. Because of you, my parents are going to move into the area to keep a close eye on me. So, thanks a lot. Thanks a fucking lot."

"Language, Dalilah," he said. "You're a well-bred lady. It would do well for you to remember that."

"Oh?" I said. "Huh. You know, I was being respectful today with Luke, and I covered up a tattoo I have on one my breasts. I covered it with my hair. I'm going to make sure that this tattoo makes it into the actual portrait now. Then you can always look upon me and remind yourself just how classy and well-bred I really am."

He looked a little bit shocked, but only for a moment. Then he smiled, and reminded me of a jack-o-lantern in doing so. "Actually, I find that rather intriguing. I would really love to see that tattoo."

I narrowed my eyes. Was this guy for real? One second, he's lecturing me about not being lady-like. The next, he's salivating over my tattoo.

"No offense, but I really don't see that ever happening."

Famous last words.

Chapter Nine

I ended up in Nottingham's penthouse that night, after drinking a few too many whiskeys. He had left me to my own devices for awhile, as I drank one shot after another. Then, at the end of the evening, he guided me gently into his limo, and, before I knew it, I was laying down on his couch.

I was in rare form, too. My eyes were crossing, and everything was spinning and blurry. I vaguely wondered if the guy had slipped some GHB, because I was feeling very woozy, even more so than usual.

"Dalilah," he said to me. "Let me see your tattoo."

I wasn't quite sure what he meant by that. Did he want me to show him, or did he want me to allow him to see it for himself? I wasn't sure, so I just laid there, and I soon found that he was unbuttoning my shirt. I laid on his couch, feeling that I couldn't move my limbs, and his hand was soon on my bra. He pulled it down, and then marveled at the little Pooh Bear tattoo that I had inked on my left breast.

"That's an adorable tattoo," he said. "Please display it in

the portrait. I believe that would so capture your essence. Your sense of whimsy and playfulness."

I wanted to tell him the real reason why I got a tattoo of the Pooh Bear. Besides the fact that the bear was always my mother's favorite, I got the tattoo to represent the childhood that I never had. I skipped right over reading about Pooh Bear, in favor of reading more complicated books such as *In Search of Lost Time* by Marcel Proust, and *Crime and Punishment* by Fyodor Dostoyevsky. Both of which were interesting, intriguing and involved, but, really, I would have liked to have been normal. So, getting the Pooh tattoo was my way of somewhat representing that which I had lost.

I didn't tell him that, though. I just nodded my head dully, and laid on the couch while he continued to undress me.

"Oh, Dalilah, you're such a beautiful woman. I don't think that you realize what you do to men who encounter you."

Oh, right. Yes, I supposed I was a quote unquote "beautiful woman." One would think that being considered beautiful and desirable would be a good thing. One would be wrong. I couldn't stand that I had so many stalkers in my life. I mean, if the right guy would stalk me, than that would be one thing. But 99.9% of the men who bugged me, and the boys, too, would fall into the category of the wrong guy. And I wasn't flattered by the attention, either. I frankly wasn't the kind of girl who would be flattered by such a thing. In other words, I didn't consider myself to be vain. So, being considered beautiful did absolutely nothing for me. Zero.

Well, unless you considered the fact that I got jobs because of the way that I looked. And well-paying ones, too. That would be the only plus to being a thing that was desired. But even that was a bit humiliating for me, because I really wanted to be making a living through my art and creativity, and that was completely extinguished. No, not extinguished. Dormant. That was a better term. Dormant. God forbid that my art ability was gone. God forbid. I didn't think that I could live for the rest of my life without it. It was bad enough living through these past 9 years without the muse guiding me.

My mind drifted, as it usually did when I was with a guy, alone. I questioned what it was that I got out of these encounters. It certainly wasn't for the sex. I didn't much get into that, to be honest. I guess because my mind was never engaged with these men and boys, and for me, even more than probably most women, I had to connect to someone intellectually before I could feel anything at all below the waist. Thus far, no member of the opposite sex, or Alaina for that matter, had been able to reach my intellect, so the sex itself was something that was a bit boring.

It certainly wasn't that I was searching for love. I knew well enough that sex, especially casual sex, wouldn't lead to love. Nor did I want it to. I had standards, even if they were double standards, and any guy who wanted to jump into bed with me, without knowing me, would not be a guy that I would want to be with in the long term.

So, what was I searching for in these encounters? Was I searching for a way to feel? To overcome my numbness? Was I just trying to not be alone? Did I fear being alone, because being alone was like death to me? After all, the only thing that I could do, when I was alone, was contemplate my failures. What was going to bring me back into the living? Sometimes I despaired that I would ever be brought back into a place where I actually felt like waking up in the morning.

I could vaguely understand that I was now naked on this man's couch. This stalker man, who I never would have thought I would be alone with, was with me, about to be on top of me, and all I could think about was when I could get out of that place and get back into my bed. Not that I was entirely unwilling. No, I would not consider this to be a rape. But I wasn't engaged, either. It was kind of a netherworld, really. A disturbing netherworld.

I took a deep breath. I tried to put it out of my mind that this man first encountered me when I was underaged, and he apparently had been obsessed with me ever since. I was Dolores Haze to his Humbert Humbert. *Lolita* was actually one of the books that I devoured when I was in kindergarten, and it was a book that I have constantly referred to in my mind, as I had encountered many, many men like this Nottingham throughout my life. Creepers, every one of them.

Not that Nottingham was particularly old. On the contrary, he appeared to be only around 30, maybe a bit older or a bit younger. But 30 would be the median that I would assume him to be. But, when he first saw me, I was apparently 18 and he was around 28. So, yeah, if you put it that way, he was a bit of a creeper.

Now, he was naked. His lips were on mine. He wasn't a bad kisser, considering. I certainly had worse in my life. His hands were caressing each of my breasts, and, then, well, he got out the handcuffs.

Oh, great, one of those guys. Well, I'll play along. Sometimes it was a little bit fun. A guy would get a bit rough, and, to my surprise, these were actually some of my favorite encounters. Probably because it wasn't the same old same old. I appreciated the creativity, if nothing else, although handcuffs were certainly pedestrian in the big scheme of things. But there was a hope that maybe this Nottingham might show a little bit of creative effort that might make this particular encounter a bit more enjoyable.

He handcuffed my hands behind me, putting the hand-cuffs behind the posts that were on the arm of the couch. It was one of those modern couches that were ever-so-slightly *avant garde*, and the arm of it was metal posts that were connected to the couch arm. He raised an eyebrow, and then did the same thing with my legs on the other couch arm.

Hmmmm, okay. Never been completely immobilized before. This might be more interesting than I initially thought. I felt myself actually start to warm up to this odd man, who really would be considered to be extraordinarily handsome by most of the world. I knew that objectively, so, if I could just concentrate on that and the fact that he had the ability to take some kind of creative initiative, I might start to enjoy myself.

I laid there, completely immobilized, wondering what was next. I was curious as to what this man might do to me now that he had me completely where he wanted me.

"Oh, Dalilah," he said, as he ran his hands completely through the length of my body. "You're so submissive. I never thought that you would be so submissive to me. Your eyes are so beautiful and passionate. I thought that you might give me a go. But you let me bind you without even a peep. You're such a contradiction. A beautiful, beautiful, contradiction."

Ha. The man actually saw passion in my eyes. Well, he was going to see what he was going to see, but I knew that there wasn't passion in my eyes, and there hadn't been in a long, long time.

"I wonder," he said. "If you would let me lay you on your stomach and bind you. I would really like to try some things with you, but I can't leave marks on your front side. That wouldn't do, because I know that Luke is going to be painting you for a long time to come."

Ooooh, marks. He wants to do something to me that is going to leave a mark. I nodded my head, and said "yes, please. I would really like that." And, I meant that. I had been roughed up before, and even had guys who were really into the sadism thing, and I didn't mind it one bit. I liked it, in fact.

And my curiosity as to exactly what this man wanted to do to me was overwhelming. So, I actually rolled over on my own and let him bind my hands and my feet, and I eagerly anticipated what was to come.

At first, I was a bit disappointed. He had taken the belt off of his pants, and whacked me a few times on my back. I felt the delicious sting, which woke me up out of my ennui, but the creativity of such an act was clearly lacking in my book. It was such a cliché, really. Rich handsome man, into whacking young women on the back with a belt.

Then, he got out the ice, and rubbed it along the parts of my back that he had clearly marked with his belt. It felt a little bit soothing, although I was quite sure that he was still trying to get me to cry out. After all, it was completely cold on my skin, and it was something that should have been totally uncomfortable. But it wasn't to me.

And then he got on top of me, plunging his manhood deep inside of me while simultaneously melting something hot on my back. I had no idea what it was, but he started licking it off while he rhythmically thrusted, so I would imagine that it wasn't hot wax. Maybe some hot fudge. In which case, I was completely envious that he wasn't going to share it with me.

Some more thwacking with the belt came next, and

some heavy-duty spanking. This guy wasn't at all trying to go easy on me. He pretty much got down to the stuff that was really painful. But I appreciated it all the same, because it was making me feel. It was waking me up and putting me in a place where I wasn't so comfortably numb.

Of course, I would have preferred to be woken up in a manner that wasn't quite so self-destructive. But it was a start.

Anal penetration, sans lube, was next. That hurt like hell. I squirmed a bit, but the pain didn't last that long. After a little while, even that was more pleasurable than painful. I felt myself breathing hard, the alcohol wearing off, along with just a bit of the veil that had been covering my emotions for this long. I started to cry out, but he tied a scarf around my mouth so that I couldn't make a sound. He thwacked my butt hard with his open hand while he plunged himself in and out, and then pulled on my hair so that my face was up in the air.

He removed the scarf from around my mouth, and eagerly started kissing me from behind. I actually started feeling something below the waist, which was something that I never thought that I would. It was tingly and warm, and the pleasurable sensation spread throughout my body. My breathing started coming heavy again, and I started groaning a little. But the groaning brought the scarf over my mouth again, and I had to suppress the urge to cry out in pleasure and pain. Which actually made the pleasurable sensation grow even more powerful. It got to the point where I really couldn't contain it, but I still had to, for I was completely silenced. Because the sensation could not be dissipated through my crying out, it grew so powerful and intense that it became almost painful. So, that pain, mingled with the general pain of the belt that was once again whacking my bare back and butt, coursed throughout my body. Waking up every cell that had been lying dormant. I could almost feel every hair on my body standing up, even moreso when Nottingham reached around to my bare breasts and clamped the nipples with something hard and metal.

That was the final straw. That pain was what made me finally started shaking my head ferociously, trying mightily to somehow will that scarf that was around my mouth to disappear. But I still couldn't cry out, so I actually felt hot tears rush down my cheeks. Which made Nottingham bring out another scarf and tie it around my eyes.

By the time he actually stopped his urgent thrusting, which signaled to me that he had his orgasm, I was actually confused about what I was feeling. But it was something that was wonderful to me, because feeling, period, was a welcome change. I was just happy that I finally felt something that was powerful enough to confuse me.

He unfastened the handcuffs on my hands and feet, and then untied both the blindfold and the gag. "Just keep laying there for a little bit, Dalilah," he said. "I'll be right back with the salve."

Oh, right. The aftercare bit. I somehow had forgotten that aftercare was supposed to be a part of the S&M ritual. It was fine, just lying there, though. I really had no desire to move. I had felt the energy drain out of my body again, and I felt myself retreating back to the shell that I was in before all of this began. Which disappointed me greatly. I had imagined, I had hoped, that the awakening that I had felt when Nottingham was inflicting pain on me was something that would somehow survive the night. That perhaps I would finally feel the tingle of excitement that I was so hoping to feel all along.

But it was not to be. I felt the veil once again cover my sensations and feelings, and I was, once again, comfortably numb. So much so that I hardly felt Nottingham's fingers gently rubbing some kind of balm on my back and butt. "Mmmm, Dalilah, you look even more delicious to me right now. It's almost like I have branded you as my own possession."

The way that he was talking to me, right at that moment, was turning me off greatly. I was no longer having the buzz that I was feeling when he was savagely tearing my flesh with his belt, so all that I could think about, right at that moment, was escaping. Getting back to my safe haven. Seeing Luke.

Seeing Luke. That popped into my head right at that moment. Why, I didn't really know. But there was something about Luke. Luke and his goofy grin, and the way that he shyly observed me while feverishly working his brush on his canvas. His cute little dimples and the cowlick that refused to behave. The gorgeous eyes that were so many different colors, and hid a fierce intelligence behind them. I could feel that emanating from him. He exuded sensuality, warmth and intelligence. Everything that this Nottingham was – cold, cruel, dominating, calculating and more than a little bit perverted – Luke appeared to be the opposite.

Nottingham continued to rub the balm into my apparent wounds on my back, and was trying to talk to me in a soothing voice. "There, there, Dalilah, this should make you feel better. Take the sting out it. My mother used to say that you should treat a burn with butter. Sounds silly, doesn't it? You have some burns on your back, and some nasty looking marks that might turn into welts. But I'm not going to use butter. I'm going to use this special salve that has aloe in it and some other ingredients which should cool every-thing down."

I finally spoke. It occurred to me that I had been partic-ularly quiet during this entire encounter. My silence no doubt amounted to acquiescence in his eyes, to everything that he was doing. Not that he would be particularly incor-rect about that, as I really was enjoying myself up until the time when he actually stopped inflicting the pain – but I really didn't consent to any of that. "Thank you, Mr. Nottingham, for putting this balm on me. And, if it's all the same to you, I would really like to just put on my clothes after you're finished with this aftercare and go on home."

His eyes flashed a look of unmistakable rage. Then he coolly, in clipped tones said "My name is Blake. Mr. Nottingham is the name of my father. And you may have your clothes when I'm ready to let you leave, and not before."

Oh, he doesn't know to whom he is speaking. Like I would ever be afraid to just go down to the lobby of his building and hail a cab, wearing nothing but a smile. Good lord, when I thought about exactly how many people, men and women, had seen me naked, mainly because I had been doing the posing thing for just under a year, even my eyes were about to cross.

"Okay," I said, rising to my feet, and grabbing ahold of my purse. "Then I guess that you leave me no choice." And, at that, I walked to his front door, completely naked, and went out into the hallway. I pushed the button for the elevator and the car was soon there to pick me up. I looked behind me, and Nottingham was running up to me, having taken the time to put his own pants on.

"Dalilah Gallagher, you get back here right now."

I flipped him off, and then pushed the button for the

elevator and made my way down. I got off the elevator, and walked through the lobby. There weren't any people down there, except for the doorman, and I saw him look at me appreciatively but furtively. I smiled at him, and pulled out my wallet and handed him a ten dollar bill. "Your tip," I said, and I made my way onto the sidewalk. Within seconds, a cab pulled up and I got in. Nottingham, of course, was right behind me, having hoofed it down the stairs, apparently, as he was out of breath. He started beating on the windows of the cab, but I simply told the driver "ignore that rather rude man. Take me to my apartment at......"

The driver kinda smiled and shook his head. He had seen it all, I was quite sure, so I was also sure that my being naked in his cab didn't really phase him too much. He pulled off the curb, and, with a screech, he started towards my destination.

I was quite sure that Nottingham would show up at my apartment in less than an hour. He first had to go back upstairs and make sure his hair looked presentable, and I was also positive that he would have to be fully dressed. Then, and only then, would he get in his car and show up at my apartment door. But, by then, it would be too late. I would already be in bed, under the covers, and I would have the deadbolt locked tight.

Of course, my prediction did come true. Because I did make my way into my apartment, and actually put on pajamas and got into bed. Within the hour, I heard Nottingham pounding on my door, but I simply got up and got some ear plugs and put them in. I could still hear the pounding and the yelling, but it was muted.

I did feel sorry for my neighbors, though.

Before I got into bed, I looked at my texts, and found one from Luke, asking me if I would mind posing the next day. I texted him back that I would be there with bells on, and I could feel the nascent feeling of excitement bubble up once again.

When the sun rose the next day, I looked down below, and saw that Nottingham's car was still parked out front. So, I shimmied down the fire escape, knowing that Nottingham had no doubt kept a vigil in my hallway, waiting for me to go out the front door.

Having made my way down the street level, I got on the bus, and headed down to Willets Point. To the area that resembled a war zone, and couldn't be further removed from Nottingham's gleaming penthouse with the gorgeous view of the Empire State Building.

Yet I knew that I would have much rather be in Luke's abandoned warehouse than ever step foot into Nottingham's lap of luxury, ever again.

Because Nottingham might have awakened something in me, but it wasn't authentic and it wasn't long-lasting. The feeling of being awake and somewhat alive only lasted as long as the pain of what he was doing seared my brain. I knew that I was looking for something that was much more permanent than that.

And, somehow, something told me that Luke might be just the person to supply this.

Chapter Ten

I got to the abandoned warehouse where I was to sit for another session with Luke. It was something that I actually was quite looking forward to, really, even though I had no idea exactly why that would be. I hardly knew this Luke. There was no reason why I thought that he might be different from any other guy who I've encountered, most of whom had, thus far, looked at me as if I was a piece of rare sirloin steak. Like the cartoons I used to watch when I was very small, and actually could appreciate them. The ones where the men were in a lifeboat or something, and they looked at each other and saw a chicken leg or a filet mignon, and started to salivate. That was what I felt like, most of my life, with men. That they would be talking to me, but really imagining what I looked like naked.

Perhaps that was the underlying reason why I decided to pose nude. Cut to the chase, really. If they were so curious about what I looked like without my clothes off, then they could go right ahead and see, without all the formalities.

But, somehow, Luke seemed different. He didn't seem

like he wanted to get me into bed first thing. He was casual, insouciant. My curiosity was piqued. I was actually looking forward to getting to know him a little bit better.

I smiled to myself, as I realized that it had actually been a long time since I had looked forward to getting to know anybody better. How jaded I had become in my relatively short life. It was sad, really.

I got to where Luke's studio was, and knocked gently on the enormous wooden door. He lifted it up, and looked at me, and smiled. A genuine smile, like he was happy to see me. I found myself feeling the same about him.

He was wearing a blue button down and ratty jeans that fit his body quite nicely, really. Other than that, it did appear as if he had just gotten out of bed, as his hair was sticking up in the air with abandon, and he had a bit of a five o'clock shadow. The light was hitting his eyes in just such a way that they appeared bright green, with hints of hazel dancing around merrily. And one thing that was always nice about him was his shoes. They were brown leather and appeared new. I noticed that first about men. Their shoes. My father always said that you can tell a lot about a person by examining their footwear. You can tell if they give a damn, and Luke apparently did.

"Dalilah," he said, his grin half-cocked. "I'm delighted to see you." And then he suddenly blushed bright scarlet, and he shook his head and looked down at the floor.

I smiled back at him. "Luke, what is it? You're turning bright red."

"Oh, just embarrassed. Dalilah, delighted. Sounds like I'm trying too hard to be a stupid poet. A really lousy one at that."

Something about his reaction just then made me laugh. He seemed so silly for getting embarrassed about something like that, but, at the same time, it was... adorable.

"Are you a poet, Luke?" I asked him.

"Nah," he said. "A songwriter, maybe, but that really is a distant second to my art. Anyhow, I'm exactly not the second coming of McCartney/Lennon in that department."

"Who is?"

"True that."

I looked around a little bit, and suddenly, for some odd reason, felt a little bit self-conscious. It was almost as if I felt like I was stripping down prematurely for him. It was a weird feeling, because I had no problem doing just that the previous day.

"Well," I finally said. "I guess I better get down to it, huh?"

He nodded, and I noticed that he now had a camera in his hand. He looked down at it, like he was adjusting the lens, and I could see that he was still blushing profusely.

I went behind the divider that he had erected for me. It did seem like a silly thing, taking off my clothes behind the divider. I mean, I was getting naked for him. Who really cared if I took off my clothes behind a divider, or if I took them off right there in full view?

Still, it was a somehow a nod to old-fashioned values, in a weird way. Ladies aren't supposed to disrobe before gentlemen, until they get to know said gentleman. So, in that way, it seemed entirely appropriate to be taking off my clothes behind the divider. After all, at heart, I was a lady.

I came back out and looked at Luke. He was sitting on his stool, his long legs dangling over the side. One of his legs was swinging back and forth nervously. But, when he saw me emerge, his big smile, dimples and all, reappeared.

I wondered if I would deliberately show him my back. I had been still feeling the pain from where I beaten by Nottingham's belt. I wondered if I had welts, or at least red marks.

Truth be told, that would be what I would be interested in, if I were in Luke's shoes right now. The symbols of pain. The marks on a person's back would be what I would be drawn to highlight, if I were to do a portrait of somebody. Because everybody carried around a great deal of pain, I was finding. Sometimes that pain was right there on the skin, ready to be portrayed on an easel. Sometimes it was more hidden and masked. But I could somehow bring that out, even when the person was attempting to hide it. I could draw it out in the person's eyes, or their body language, or their demeanor. Even if the person was smiling when I painted them, there would always be something there. Something that might not be detected by the naked eye, but would be an instant connection to somebody who was experiencing sadness or hurt.

Portraits were really a small part of what I did, but I was good at them. My subjects were always quite amazed at how well I could capture their essence. Perhaps they really didn't know why I could portray them so realistically. If they didn't recognize their own damage to their psyche, which was so clearly brought into the light, then they probably couldn't quite put a finger on why it was the visage that was on the canvas spoke to them so vividly. They only knew that it did somehow.

My ability to recognize pain in others, and portray it well, was really my secret weapon. It was also the reason why I was so in demand for awhile. Well, that, coupled with the sheer novelty of seeing a small child paint them with accuracy, precision and a certain degree of abandon.

My intuition had always served me well in that regard.

I took a deep breath, wondering if I should reveal that part of myself to Luke so soon. That damaged part that was now shown so clearly on my skin.

But then I thought better of it. There was no need to let this kind, talented and extraordinarily handsome man know the depths of my freakitude on the second day of knowing him.

So, I just laid down on the fainting couch, being very careful to only show my front side to him.

He smiled and sat down at his easel. "Are you comfortable enough?" he asked me.

"Very," I said.

So, for the next hour or so, Luke sat behind his easel. He studied me for about twenty minutes or so, his hand on his chin. And then he would start his hand working furiously for another twenty minutes or so, then it would start all over again. I knew why he was working with so much more abandon the first time, and why, this time, it all seemed so painstaking. I appreciated that he was pondering the details, and how to portray them properly. When it came down to the minutiae, it was always difficult and took a lot of thinking.

Finally, he stretched a little bit. "I need a break," he said. "And you probably do, too. Why don't you put your clothes on for a little bit, if you don't mind, and we can have some lunch or something? I mean, if you don't have pressing plans."

"Actually, that sounds lovely," I said, trying to tamp down my rising sense of excitement over seeing Luke somewhat socially. To my own dismay, I felt the blood rushing to my own cheeks. Luke looked at me a little bit quizzically, as if he was wondering why it was that I would feel the need to blush.

I was wondering that one myself.

I stood up, and Luke turned around modestly. As if he were saying that he wanted to give me my privacy as I made my way behind the divider. That relieved me, because I was realizing, more and more, that I had no desire for Luke to see my backside. There was something about what had happened last night, between Nottingham and me, which had made me feel ashamed. Almost dirty. And it wasn't even that I participated in off-color sex games. It was that I was having sex at all with somebody that I hardly knew.

And that feeling, that sleeping with a stranger was somehow wrong, was alien to me. I had never before seen it in that light. I didn't know why it never had occurred to me that sex should be something that is between two people who actually have feelings for one another. It just never did.

Until right at that moment, that is.

I threw on my clothes and boots, and walked back in front of the divider. "I'm ready," I said. "Where would you like to go?"

"Uh, there's a little diner that's down the street a little bit. It's actually within walking distance. I know, this area doesn't seem like there is any kind of real civilization around, but the workers have to eat somewhere. And it's pretty damned good food too. If you don't mind a greasy spoon."

"I love greasy spoons," I told him. Which was true. Growing up with wealthy parents didn't mean that I wasn't exposed to the more mundane things in life, such as greasy spoons. That was because my parents were surprisingly down to earth, considering how much money they had. Especially my mother. She always struck me as the working-class-girl-made-good that she actually was. Nothing in the intervening years, between her meeting my father and today, had changed that about her. Something about taking a girl out of a working class neighborhood, but never taking the working class neighborhood out of the girl.

I was startled as I realized that I actually had an endearing thought about my mother, which was a rarity, in and of itself. I suddenly could see that I was always too hard on her, because I always was thinking that she couldn't understand or relate to me. Perhaps I could accept her more, and her limitations, and try to find common ground.

As I walked along with Luke, through the sidewalks that were littered with beer bottles and various other sundry items, I marveled about how my attitudes towards people in my life, and life in general, was starting to shift. The shift was still imperceptible, and threatening to recede, much like my newfound *joie de vivre* from the previous night had receded as soon as my little games with Nottingham were through. But, at the same time, the shift was there. Perhaps if I nurtured it a little it could come into full bloom.

After a few blocks of walking, we came upon a small restaurant that looked like it was housed in a converted trailer. On the roof was a neon sign that blared the words "Joey's Diner." We walked into the rather small place, where there was a cook behind the counter with a white hat on. The guy looked like a typical diner owner from the movies and television – around 50 years old, slightly pudgy, short and craggy. He was joking around with two or three people who sat around the counter, eating typical greasy spoon type food – eggs and hash, some kind of meat smothered in gravy with a side of mashed potatoes, and hamburgers.

The guy lit up when he saw us coming through the door.

"Luke, my boy! How you been?" The guy had a thick "New Yawk" type accent and a very jolly demeanor.

Luke put his arm around my shoulder, which gave me a strange sensation of shivers coursing throughout my body. I looked at Luke, wondering where those shivers and little butterflies, which were forming in my stomach, were coming from. "Just great, Joey. Hey, Joey, this is Dalilah Gallagher. Dalilah, this is Joey Facinelli."

I put out my hand for Joey to shake, but he came around and gave Luke and me a big bear hug instead. "Any friend of Luke is a friend of mine," he said with a hearty laugh. Then he turned to Luke. "What's a guy look you doing with a classy girl like this?"

"Just lucky I guess," Luke said, not bothering to correct Joey's apparent perception that I was Luke's date.

Not that I minded being thought of as Luke's date. I didn't mind at all.

Luke and I sat at the counter, and Joey got back behind it and said "okay, then, what can I do you for? The usual?"

Luke nodded. "Yep, the usual. Hamburger with everything and large fries. And Dalilah would like…" At that, he turned and looked at me. "So sorry, Dalilah, I didn't think to find out what you like to eat."

I nodded at Joey. "A hamburger and fries sounds good to me too." I then looked over to Luke, who was staring back at me in appreciation. "What?" I said to Luke teasingly. "I would have ordered the caviar, but I just had that for breakfast." Then I smiled, as I took a sip of the water that was just brought out.

He smiled back, his dimples making me feel a little bit weak in the knees. "Ah, too bad. Joey's caviar is the best in town. The lobster, too."

At that, I surreptitiously looked at the menu, just to check and make sure that there actually wasn't lobster or caviar on the menu. I knew that Luke was joking, but I always liked to check anyhow. Then I looked up, and Luke was staring at me, his eyes dancing. He grinned crookedly, and said "aw, come on, you didn't really believe that a greasy joint like this would have lobster and caviar, did ya?"

I laughed, feeling a bit foolish for falling for the joke for even a second. "Of course not," I said. "Silly."

Then he nudged my leg with his under the counter. It was a flirtatious move, and I felt the shivers course through my body again. *What the hell was wrong with me?*

"So, Luke," Joey was saying. "How'd you come out with the ponies yesterday?"

Luke looked embarrassed and ran his hand through his hair. I smiled at his seeming uncomfortable about betting on a horse race, although I longed to let him know that I was perfectly okay with that. I had played my share of blackjack myself, and had actually gotten pretty good at it. Of course, it was partially due to my ability to count cards, no matter how many decks they had in the shoe, so my conscience eventually got the better of me and I started playing without doing that. Once I started losing, I decided that it wasn't the game for me after all.

"Not bad at all," he said. "I actually won fifty bucks."

"Ah, then, I guess you're buying, huh?" Joey said with a hearty laugh.

"Yeah, something like that." He still looked embarrassed, and he sipped his water, not meeting my eyes. So, I put my arm around his shoulders and smiled at him. He brought his eyes up to meet mine, his crooked grin with the cute dimples back.

Joey addressed me. "So, I guess I didn't ask you this, but what would you like to drink besides water?"

"Um, some iced tea would be great," I said.

Joey looked at Luke. "I'm guessing you want the usual, huh?"

"Yeah. A suicide."

"Coming right up."

I looked at my straw and said "you know, I've always wondered why they call mixing up a bunch of drinks a suicide. I mean, really, it's not that deadly, is it?"

"Well, of course it is," Luke said. "All pop is deadly, really. It rots your belly. But I know what you mean. I've been drinking suicides ever since I was a kid and they started having those self-serve pop machines in every fast food joint."

"Me too," I said. "I got that from my mom, I guess. She always liked doing that."

Luke smiled "your mom. Does she live around here? I have noticed that you don't have an East Coast accent at all." Luke's own accent didn't exactly seem New York, but someplace East Coast. Maine, maybe. I remembered going to some of the seafood towns around the Maine coasts, when I traveled with Nick and Scotty and their kids. The fishermen who worked around those places sounded just like Luke.

I shook my head. "Kansas City. She was raised there, anyhow. So was I until I was 17."

Luke narrowed his eyes at me. "17, huh? And that was how many years ago that you came here?"

I laughed. "If you want to know my age, I'll just tell you. I'm 20. I just had a birthday in August, so I just turned 20 a couple of months ago."

"20. So, how do you get into bars?"

"How do you know I go to bars?"

He shrugged. "I don't know, I just figured that you do."

"Well," I said. "I have a fake ID." At that, I brought it out for him to see.

He nodded his head, evidently impressed. "Very authentic, Deanna Cerino," he said, reading the name on the ID. "But you don't much look Italian." And then he smiled and handed the ID back to me.

"What?" I said. "You seem surprised that I would have a fake ID."

"Nah, not surprised," he said. "I mean, who doesn't when they're under 21? Except me, of course. I'm one of the dorks who doesn't know somebody who can help me get one."

I was wondering how old Luke was, and he just answered my question. Sort of.

"And you are?" I asked.

"I'm also 20. But I turn 21 in December, so I know what I will be doing."

"So, how do you bet on the horse races if you're not 21?"

"Oh, that's easy. My uncle lives in upstate New York, and I just give the money to him. He's really the only family member that I trust not to cheat me, though. As sad as that is."

Just then, Joey brought our food out to us. I dug into my burger, which was actually delicious. Perhaps the best I had ever had. It was crispy on the edges, and juicy in the middle. It just had the basics on it – ketchup, mustard and pickles. The fries were just as good – crispy and brown, with just the right amount of salt on them.

"So, what do you think?" Luke asked me, as he took bites out of his own burger.

"Delicious," I said. "These little restaurants always do have the best food."

"Nah, this isn't a restaurant," Luke said. "It's a joint. You can call it that. Joey won't get upset, right Joey?"

"This ain't no joint," he said, indignantly. "It's a fine dining establishment. Too bad you didn't come in when my maître d' was here. He gets here at 5."

Luke smiled at Joey and winked. "Hey, at least I didn't call this place what it is. The 'd' word."

"The 'd' word?" I asked. "You mean dive?"

"Shhhh, never say that word out loud around Joey. He turns green and bursts out of his clothes when people call this place that word."

To which Joey said "yeah, this place is a dive. What of it?"

I smiled and said "well, dive or no dive, this is the best goddamned hamburger I have ever had."

Both Luke and Joey momentarily looked at me with a bit of shock, and then both of them started laughing.

"Hey, the next thing you know," Joey was saying to Luke. "This little girl is going to be finishing the Joey special."

"The Joey special?" I asked, and then looked at where Joey was pointing. The sign detailed what the 'Joey Special' was. It was apparently four lbs of beef, with all the trimmings on it – lettuce, pickle, tomato and special sauce. It was served with three pounds of French fries, and the sign said that anybody who could finish it all in under a half hour not only got it for free, but also got their picture on the wall.

Thus far, there were only three pictures on the wall. All

of the pictures showed men who looked rather green and about to puke. "Hmmm, I'm guessing not too many people are successful in completing that challenge, from the looks of things."

"You might say that," Luke said. "I tried one time, and got halfway through that gut-bomb of a burger and cried uncle. Loudly. But, I'm never one to back away from a challenge, so I'm going to try, try again."

"Yeah," Joey said. "Great ambition in this kid, there. Finish my special and get his name on the wall."

Luke just smiled and Joey punched him lightly on the arm. "I'm just giving you crap. You know I love you. The proof is there on that other wall."

I looked around at where Joey's eyes were, and there on the wall was an exquisite impressionistic painting of a nearly abandoned city street. The use of color, light and brush strokes, combined with the technique, made me gasp. The trees were multi-colored, but mainly burnt orange, and the street shimmered with a multi-colored hue that made the entire painting seem to undulate. There was a sense of alienation that was perfectly captured on the canvas, as shown by the lone figure on the sidewalk with non-descript features. There were shades of Guillaumin in this painting, as it depicted the sense of foreboding in the modern landscape.

I looked back at Luke, who was blushing eight shades of scarlet. I cocked my head at him. "You did that?" I asked, gesturing to the painting on the wall.

He shrugged and turned almost purple. "It's not very good, I know. I mean, it's nothing like yours."

I sucked my drink down with my straw, and watched him from my side-eye. His work really was magnificent. Raw, with perfect technique and really captured the essence of how I saw the city myself. I found myself feeling profoundly impressed, yet a little bit envious. "It's gorgeous," I said. "But how do you know about my work?"

"I Googled you, of course. I mean, you didn't say as much, but I figured that you were an art student or something. Needless to say, I found your images on-line. They were beyond words. You have a talent that far surpasses mine or anybody else I know. My stuff looks positively banal next to yours."

"I think that you don't have a sense of your own talent," I said. "And, for the record, I don't paint anymore. I'm guessing you figured that out for yourself, though, considering none of those paintings were created within the last nine years."

"Yeah," he said. "I also found the review by that son of a bitch Jacobs, too. Where the hell does he get off spouting off that obviously biased bullshit? I have no idea whose work he thought he was critiquing, but 'stale, derivative and lifeless' would be the last three words that I would ever use to describe your work."

I felt myself retreating at just the mention of that man's name. "Let's not talk about that, okay?" I said. "I want to enjoy my lunch."

"Oh, sure," he said, obviously feeling embarrassed about his display of pique over my devastating review. "Sorry about that. I just got so worked up last night when I was reading it. But won't bring it up again."

We ate in silence for a few minutes, as I finished off the burger and fries, dragging the fries around the ketchup on the plate. I felt bad for shutting down the conversation about my work, but it was still such a touchy subject with me. I did, however, want to find out more about Luke. His talent was phenomenal, much more than he would ever admit or perhaps even see.

So, I made a mental note to myself to try to do some Googling of my own that evening.

Perhaps I finally found something more interesting than getting schnockered.

Chapter Eleven

Luke

That same night, after I took Dalilah out to my little hole in the wall that had the best damned food in the Queens borough, or presumably did, I went home and tried to stay out of trouble. I could feel myself becoming ashamed about the badges of my working-class background when I was around Dalilah. Somehow, Joey just couldn't resist embarrassing me, no matter how classy the girl was who I was with, which was why he had made a point about my betting on the horses. But Dalilah didn't need to know about the little gambling I did. Not that it was a big deal. It was just a few horse races here and there, and a weekly poker game with the guys. I never lost more than $100 at a time, mainly because I just couldn't afford to do so. Besides, my horse race bets were pretty sound, as I always, always did my homework on the ponies. That way my losses were minimized.

Even so, I somehow didn't want her to know that I ever

gambled at all. I had no idea why that was so embarrassing for me, except maybe to think that Dalilah was so rarefied that she would never deign to be with a working-class guy like myself. And I was trying hard to present myself as somebody who was more in her league. As fruitless as that was.

It didn't help that I had Googled the girl and spent most of the previous evening reading about her and her life. She was fucking famous when she was a child. She was a prodigy that had been featured in just about every art magazine there was, and there was even an article about her in *Time* magazine. She was referred to as the "Mozart of the art world," because she had such a sophisticated aesthetic at such a young age.

My intimidation about her grew as I studied her work online. She was goddamned amazing. She had dabbled in many different genres, from surrealism to impressionism, while her portraits were perfect examples of realism. They were almost hyper-realistic, for her details were so painstaking that it was difficult to tell her portraits apart from actual photographs. Yet she had a knack for bringing out the emotions behind the subject's eyes. I could almost read the thoughts of the people that she painted, for she was that talented in portraying their essence.

But it was her work in urban expressionism that really drew me in. She evidently was gravitating towards that genre when she quit, as this was the genre that was represented in her major showings that she garnered when she was just 10 years old. It was amazing to me how clear-eyed she was in viewing the world, considering her tender age, and how she was able to portray it through her use of color, light and form. I could easily read what she was trying to say, and that was that the world was screwed-up, and she used her work to express how she felt about such issues as poverty, racism, alienation, animal rights, and environmental ethics. As abstract as her message was, I got it. I got her. Her art told me everything that I needed to know about her, and that was that she was an extremely gifted, intelligent and sensitive soul.

Which was why I felt like tearing Jacobs a new asshole when I read his scathing review of her showing at the *Luhring.* I was livid, reading what he had to say about her. I couldn't understand, at all, why this art critic would publish something that was obviously so biased. Anybody with half a brain could understand that Dalilah was a rare talent. Anybody. Yet this asshole acted as if she was some kind of second-rate hack.

Then I read more about Jacobs, and it all became clear. He apparently has a daughter who was a struggling artist. She was around 20 years old when Dalilah was getting her major showings. His daughter was also trying to get recognition in the genre of urban expressionism. It seemed to me to be a classic case of tearing down the competition. As unprofessional as that was for an art critic to do that, it seemed to be the only logical explanation. I could just imagine how an 11 year old would feel, seeing her work torn like that in such a savage and scathing manner. No wonder she quit. She had the talent of somebody twice her age, but the maturity level of a child.

I only hoped that she could overcome her mental blocks and start painting again. The world needed someone like her, and for her to be cowering in the background, when she clearly should be front and center and creating a major name for herself in the art world, would be absolutely a tragedy and a waste. It would be as if Basquiat had quit before he was able to compose the masterpieces that he did.

It was tragic enough that Basquiat died at the age of 27, the same age as so many other great artists and singers, but if he had quit art at the age of 11, that would have been an even worse tragedy.

So, Dalilah was an enigma. A fascinating, beautiful enigma. Who also came from an extraordinarily wealthy family. I found that out as well in my Googling. Which was part of the reason why I was feeling the need to hide my own working-class background. As silly as it sounded to try to cover up who I was, as she was going to find out, sooner or later, I still felt the need to try to make her think that I was at least somewhat her equal. If only so that she could trust me to do a good job with her portrait.

I tried to put it out of my mind that she and I could ever be something more. As much as I was drawn to her, I just couldn't see something like that ever happening. So, I had made up my mind that it was not something that I would ever try to pursue.

Just then, my phone started ringing. It was Jake, who was my best buddy. He and I often hung out, and he was a part of my weekly poker game as well. Sometimes he was my baking buddy, and other times we would just get together and listen to music and shoot the shit. At that moment, he had been involved with a rather stunning restaurant hostess, and they had been hot and heavy. So, I hadn't actually seen him in quite awhile.

"Hey," I said. "What's up?"

"Dude," he said. "I just got dumped."

"Crap. When?"

"Just now. Wanna hang out?"

"Sure." Why not? I wasn't working that evening, and my latest work in progress, which was a surrealistic view of

Times Square, wasn't exactly going swimmingly. Maybe it was time for a little brew and commiseration.

"Meet you at the b-ball court," he said.

"On my way."

So, I got on my jacket and shorts, got my battered basketball out of my closet, and headed down to the court that we always played in. Hopefully there wouldn't be a game going on there already, so that Jake and I might actually be able to get a game going. I was a decent player, and Jake was excellent, so I usually looked forward to these matches. I always wanted somebody to push me, so that I could become better, even when it came to something as ultimately inconsequential to my life as basketball.

A short bus ride later, and I was on the court with Jake. He looked like he wasn't having that great of day. His hair, which was normally a nicely combed dark wavy brown, was going in every direction. He had bags under his eyes, and he looked like he hadn't slept for quite awhile.

He said that he was just dumped, but, from the looks of it, it seemed as if it had been coming for a long time.

The yard was deserted, as it was still in the middle of the day, so he saw me and nodded, and I tossed the ball in the air. Both of us leaped up to gain control of the ball, with Jake getting the ball and he immediately started dribbling down the court.

For the next half hour or so, we played a rough and tumble game. I was better at defense than he was, and he was clearly better at shooting. As I was only marginally better on defense than him, he usually was able to school me on the court. But he didn't on that day. I was getting into better shape all the time, as I had taken up running and lifting weights, so I was able to keep up with him, shot for shot.

We finally quit the game to take a break, with him leading me by a basket. We sat down and got a drink of water, both of us out of breath and sweating. Jake playfully shook his head, the sweat beads flying through the air and landing on my shirt.

"Gross, dude," I said, and then tried to do the same to him, but not quite managing it. My hair was just too short for that, I guess, although I certainly didn't have a buzz cut. If anything, I think that I was overdue for a haircut.

He tossed the ball at me, and we got up another game. He started a conversation while we played. "So," he said, while he dribbled the ball as I tried to get it away from him. "Belinda called me today to tell me that things just weren't working out. For whatever reason. I don't know, bro, I thought things were going okay. Not sure what I was missing."

"Sometimes it happens that way," I said. I, of all my buddies, was often the one who was called upon to size up romantic issues, simply because I was known as the 'sensitive' one of the bunch. In other words, I understood women much better than did any of them, which wasn't saying a whole lot. "Women put out a lot of non-verbal cues. We just have to get better at picking up on them."

"Yeah?" he said. "Like what?"

"I don't know what," I said. "It's like porn. I know 'em when I see 'em." I was paraphrasing Supreme Court Justice Potter Stewart, in a pornography case, where he wrote that famous line regarding how to tell if something is pornographic. I thought the same thing about the intangibles like the non-verbal cues that women give off when they're ready to jump. I was never wrong about it, either. I was always astounded that my buddies couldn't pick up on the same things, though. What was always obvious to me, somehow never was to them.

"Shit, dude, you're going to have to do better than that."

As I dribbled the ball, I thought of an example. "Okay," I said. "Remember that one girl that you hit up at the bar about a month ago or so. Right before you met Belinda?"

"Narrow it down, bro, I hit up a lot of girls in the bar." There was a bar that Jake and I went to that never carded anybody, and was constantly getting shut down because of it. But that place made so much money out of serving minors, it was well worth it to have to be shut down once in awhile.

"Okay," I said. "Actually, this is something that happens all the time. Don't get me wrong, you're a good-looking guy, but sometimes you get all up on some woman who clearly doesn't want nothing to do with you."

He shot me a dirty look, and I shrugged. "It happens," I said. "Anyhow, I distinctly remember this one girl. You were talking to her, hanging on her, and she was all talking to her girlfriends while you were trying to get her attention. I think that you were clueless that she wasn't picking up what you were throwing down."

He looked mystified. Granted, he was kind of a stud, really. He got a lot of women, most of them pretty smoking, so pointing out his rather rare mis-fires probably was a blow to his ego.

Finally he shrugged. "Eh, she probably already had a boyfriend."

"I'm sure that she did," I said. I ran down the court, and dunked the ball, and then chased Jake down the court while he dribbled and he finally shot a basket from half-court, making it through the hoop cleanly.

"Nothing but net, my brother," he said, putting his hand down as I slapped it. "Let's go get a brew and shoot some pool."

We both changed in the bathroom, and headed down to our bar in his beater hoopdie Corolla. "When are you going to get some wheels?" he asked me in the car.

I thought about it, realizing that, with Nottingham's money, getting a car might be a distinct possibility. Of course, I hadn't actually seen dime one from Nottingham, so the car would just have to wait. Unless I wanted an absolute hoopdie that constantly had to be worked on, which Jake did, in his own driveway, just about every week. Personally, I had better things to do with my time than mess around with a car that was constantly on its last gasp, as was Jake's Corolla, which was nicknamed Brown Betty.

"Fuck that, man," I said. "You know I'm looking to move to the city soon. No use getting a car now."

Jake started laughing. "You've been talking about moving to the city ever since I've known you. Unless you suddenly got some kind of sugar momma, I don't see that move happening, my brother."

I bristled at the words *sugar momma*. "The only momma I've been getting with is your momma. Last night, in fact."

"Ha ha ha," he said with a roll of his eyes. "Seriously, man, you gotta hustle your shit more. You're really good. I'm just busting ya when I tease you about not being able to move to the city. You gotta cash in that lotto ticket you were born with, sooner or later."

I shook my head. Heard it all before. Truth be told, before Nottingham, nobody even really noticed me. It was tough standing out amongst all the wickedly talented artists who were in this city.

We ordered our beers, and Jake looked around the bar.

He caught the eye of a willowy blonde who was there with three of her girlfriends, and excused himself to go over and talk to her.

He certainly did work fast.

I looked at my phone, feeling bored and wanting to bolt. Which I would, if Jake ended up with blondie. I casually texted Dalilah, not really sure exactly why I was doing so. She just seemed to creep into my thoughts, just when I wasn't expecting it. It wasn't even her beauty or her talent or her obvious intelligence. It was something else, something that was as intangible as the non-verbal cues that I was discussing with Jake on the b-ball court.

"Hey there, Dalilah," I said, almost as a joke, as I knew that I was ripping off the ubiquitous song from many years ago.

She texted me back immediately, an emoticon smile. "Oh, what you do to me," she wrote, obviously continuing the joke. "How are you tonight, Luke?"

"Awesome," I texted. "What's up your way?"

"Doing some Googling," she texted back. "Found your website."

I felt a little bit embarrassed, although I really didn't know why. There was something about Dalilah seeing all of my work that made me feel vaguely uncomfortable, as if she would see it and find it wanting somehow. "Oh, yeah? Bet you couldn't tell my work apart from Matisse, huh?"

Another emoticon smile. "I'm actually VERY impressed," she texted. "Your use of color and light is very reminiscent of Michael Flohr," she texted, referring to the modern impressionist whose work I really did admire. "But you aren't derivative, either. Your style is certainly unique."

I smiled, hoping that she wasn't blowing smoke up my ass. "Well, it's nothing compared to yours," I texted.

She sent a frowny face emoticon to that. "No, much better."

I was just about to send her another text, when she sent another one of her own. "Would you like to come over and watch a movie?" she texted.

I was somewhat startled, as I wasn't expecting that. I rapidly texted "what time?"

"As early as you can get here."

I glanced over at Jake, who was engrossed in conversation with blondie, and probably wouldn't ever notice that I had high-tailed it out of there. "Be there in an hour," I texted, regretting telling her that somewhat, as I knew that I had to shower before getting on the subway and the bus to get to where she was in SoHo. "What's your addy?" I texted, realizing that I had no idea where she lived, except that it was in SoHo somewhere.

She texted it, and then wrote "I'll order Chinese delivery. What's your poison?"

"Anything moo shoo," I texted. "But I'm easy when it comes to Chinese. Surprise me."

"Will do."

I put my phone away with a smile, looking way forward to that evening, much more so than I had ever looked forward to anything else prior to that. There was something about this girl....

I went over to Jake, who was now draped over blondie, who didn't seem to mind one bit. "Cutting out," I said to him. "Catch you later, huh?"

"Yeah, later," he said.

I leaned over to whisper to him. "Just for the record, this is the kind of body language you want," I said, gesturing to blondie, who was leaning into him and smiling.

"I'll remember that," he said.

At that, I went to catch the bus to my apartment, so that I could make my way to see Dalilah.

Chapter Twelve

Dalilah

I got off my texting with Luke, and was awaiting him coming over to hang out with me. It was a spur of the moment decision to invite him over, inspired by the fact that I really, really, really wanted to see him. Especially after I Googled him and saw how talented he really was. His website showed paintings and sculptures that were really a stroke of genius. He showed clear influences of the masters of his field, but, at the same time, he took a fresh perspective and was able to bring this unique perspective to the subjects that he chose. There was desolation and loneliness right there on the canvas, but there was also a sense of hope and optimism. I could sense the hope and optimism when I was with him, as he was very good-natured and upbeat. But I wondered about what was underneath the facade, too, and was intrigued to say the very least.

There was definitely more to him than what met the eye. Of that, I was sure. I had always had amazing intuition about people, and I credited my father for that. He could get a read on anybody in a split second. What made them tick. What they feared. How they were inspired. My father had a sensitivity and a depth that was missing from most men, and I always admired him for this. Genetically, I definitely had much more in common with my dad than with my mother. She was a lovely person, but more than a little bit obtuse sometimes.

I felt little butterflies, and more than a little bit girlie as I fussed over myself in mirror. Perhaps it was time to upgrade my wardrobe, I thought with a bit of consternation, as I searched for a cute top or skirt, but then realized that I had nothing in my drawers and closet but jeans, t-shirts, frumpy sweaters and wooly boots. Alaina's nagging voice rang in my ears about how I needed to get with it in the clothes department. She had tried to drag me to Bergdorf, Barney's and Bloomingdales more times than I cared to count, but, every time, I went along just to get lunch and an ice-cream cone, and failed to pick up so much as a colorful scarf during these excursions.

I guess I was just a tomboy at heart, really. That, and the fact that I failed to get the boy-crazy fever that swept Alaina, Janelle, and virtually every other female I knew. So, for me to suddenly be obsessing over my wardrobe and getting butterflies over some boy was a feeling that was alien to me. Not an entirely unwelcome feeling, mind you. Just alien.

After about ten minutes of deciding upon whether I should wear a white t-shirt or a blue one or one of my t-shirts that had a smartass message on it, I decided to call Alaina. She had recently moved into my building, which was both a good thing and a bad thing. Good because I could pretty much go and see her whenever I wanted to, provided that she was home, which she often wasn't. Bad because you can sometimes get sick of seeing a person. Not that I was yet sick of seeing her. But I could imagine a time in the near future when I would be.

"Alaina," I said, after she miraculously answered the phone. "Do you have anything I could borrow?"

She started laughing. "I told you. I told you that you would want to borrow clothes from me sometime. Sure, come on down and pick some stuff out. But, next time I take you shopping, could you please buy something for yourself?"

I was about to open my mouth to remind her that I was trying, very hard, to not rely on my parents for money, therefore shopping at high-end places was not realistic for me, but then thought better of it. That was a constant source of arguments between Alaina and me. She clearly thought that I should let my parents support me, at least until I became the famous artist that she was still convinced I was going to be. I, on the other hand, could not have imagined anything more humiliating. Perhaps if I were in school, as Alaina was, I would have thought differently about the subject. But I wasn't. I chose to come to New York City to make my own mark in the world, and staying here on my parent's dime didn't quite factor into my some-what romantic notion I had about my future in the city.

I went down the stairs to Alaina's one-bedroom apartment that was clearly much larger than my little studio. Alaina could also afford to decorate her place with something other than hand-me-downs, so she had the best of everything. She had a funky aesthetic, favoring colorful blue and yellow couches that contrasted with the salmon-colored curtains. Yet everything seemed to blend. Her ceilings were around 12 feet high, so the place seemed enormous, really, and there was plenty of natural light that streamed through her large windows. Not that there was any light coming through the windows right then, of course - it was around 6 o'clock, and the sun was setting early, as it was early October. So, the apartment was lit up with various colorful floor lamps and some overhead track lighting.

She opened the door. "Come on in, Dalilah. I'm happy to see you, by the way. You haven't been around much lately."

"Yeah, I've been busy. Sorry about that." Of course, that was a lie. I wasn't busy with anything but being a slutty barfly. I hoped that was about to change, though.

I went into her bedroom, and she gestured to her walk-in closet. "What's mine is yours. Lucky for you that we're the same size."

I smiled and nodded, and selected a silk blouse and a mini-skirt, with thigh-high boots. Without thinking, I took off my sweater in front of Alaina, and turned around when I heard her gasp.

"What the fuck?" she asked me, touching my back. "What the hell happened to you?"

I felt my face turn about fourteen shades of purple, as I realized what she was looking at. Alaina was now going to be privy to my freakitude, and I wasn't liking that prospect one bit. "Uh," I said. "I don't want to go into that right now. Luke is due at my apartment at any moment now."

"Did he do this to you?" she demanded. Her hands were on her hips, and I think that I knew what was next. She would tell my parents, and then there would be hell to pay. Not that Alaina was a snitch, but she was a good friend, and, as a good friend, if I was involved in an abusive relationship, I was quite sure that she would try to get me help. Which would necessarily involve telling my mom and dad.

Which was the last thing that I wanted. I was skating on thin ice with them as it was. Not that they could do anything, legally, as I was an adult. But they certainly could make my life hell by incessantly prying and spying. Not to mention the fact that they probably would enlist Nick to come over here to kick my ass. My sweet dad was scary enough when he was angry. Nick – whoo boy, I didn't want to get on his wrong side. Nice guy, but could be a total bad-ass when he wanted to be.

I tried to think fast, but lying was never my strong suit. So, I just told her the truth. "No, no, no. Luke is a nice boy. But I kinda ended up with this kinky guy who was into this kind of thing. I don't anticipate ever seeing him again in that way, although I'm quite sure that I will see him again in some capacity. He's kinda a stalker."

"A stalker," she said. "What's his name?"

"Blake Nottingham," I said.

At that, she sat down on her chair. "Fuck. Who knew a guy like that would be such a perv?"

"Do you know him?"

"I know of him. Of course. Who doesn't? He owns half of lower Manhattan. Bars, restaurants, and more than a few galleries. If you ever start your art career again, he would be a great contact for you. But I don't suggest that you see him again socially if he's into all that. I mean, fuck. He really did a number on you."

I felt embarrassed, not knowing that Nottingham was that powerful and wealthy. I mean, I knew that he was powerful and wealthy, but I didn't know that he was into all those different businesses. Including galleries. I made a mental note to Google him when Luke left. Perhaps I could use him to get more work for Luke. There wasn't any reason why Luke had to struggle the way that he did, when he was so goddamned talented.

"Here," Alaina said as she handed me a bracelet, a wary look on her face. "Borrow this. And I can see your wheels turning, Dalilah. I was kidding when I suggested that you use Nottingham as a contact. He sounds kinda wacked. But, then again, there's lots of guys who are into that. I just didn't imagine that you'd be involved with any of them."

"I'm not involved. It was only that one night." I looked down at my wrist, which was adorned with Alaina's shiny bracelet. "I'm not into that. I mean, I kinda liked it, because it woke me up a bit. But I think it's destructive, and I don't want to go down that path. So, you can rest assured that I won't be with him anymore."

"I hope not," she said. "I mean, light bondage and spanking is one thing. This is something else entirely."

I nodded my head. "Well, thanks for letting me borrow these things, Alaina. Maybe when I finally get my art going again, and I can afford to shop at these high-end places, I can return the favor to you."

"Well, until then, you can feel free to take as many clothes as you like without having to return them. Not that I think of you as a charity case, because god knows you're not, but I do understand your wanting to be independent from your parents. And I take clothes into the thrift stores all the time. Maybe I'll just bring them to you instead."

I smiled. That actually sounded like a great arrangement, especially since Alaina really had amazing taste. And I knew that she wasn't lying when she said that she took her clothes to the thrift store all the time. She tired of things easily, so she hauled stuff over to Goodwill and the Salvation Army just about every month. "Thanks," I said. "I would appreciate that."

"Don't mention it," she said. "And Dalilah?"

"Yeah?"

"Stay away from that guy. He sounds like a creeper."

"He *is* a creeper. And, don't worry, I won't get sexually involved with him again."

"Good. I don't like seeing those welts and bruises on you. I'm sorry, I know that lots of people are into that, and they're not all messed up. But he did that without really knowing if you wanted it, it sounds like. Give that guy the slip."

"I will."

At that, I left her apartment and made my way up to my own apartment to wait for Luke. Nottingham was far from my mind as I made my way up the steps and then opened the door to my apartment. I could only think of that cute boy with the dimples and messed-up hair, who had layers and depth that I was really anxious to uncover.

Chapter Thirteen

Before Luke got to my apartment, there was a matter of calling for the promised Chinese takeout. I ordered the Moo Shoo chicken, and the garlic shrimp. I felt a little bit guilty about eating meat and seafood, because I was raised a vegan. After all, my parents were animal-rights activists. But I tried to put the plight of the animals out of my mind as I waited for the takeout to arrive.

Luke actually arrived before the takeout, though. My heart skipped a beat, or maybe a thousand beats, as I opened up the door after buzzing him up. He looked unusually handsome in his green sweater and jeans, with his shoes looking their usual shiny selves. Because of the shade of his sweater, the green in his eyes seemed to dominate more than usual, but I knew that if I looked at him in another light, the eyes would change color like they usually did.

He looked just a bit shy, as he offered me a bouquet of wild flowers. He blushed crimson as he said "Uh, I picked these up. I mean, I hope that I wasn't presumptuous that this is a date, or anything, but I just thought that you might like them."

I smiled at his awkwardness. I felt just as awkward, as even I didn't necessarily know if this was considered to be a date. I mean, we were hanging out that night. And I actually wanted it to be a date. But it was still kind of a grey area. So, I just decided to thank him and not try to confirm that this was considered to be a date. "Thanks, Luke. These are gorgeous. I'll have to find a vase to put them in. Wait right there and make yourself comfortable. Would you like wine or something else to drink?"

"Sure, whatever you're drinking."

I went into my tiny kitchen and produced a vase and filled it with water, and then tried to find a suitable wine. Fortunately, wine was something that I knew a lot about. After all, my dad owned a winery in Italy. So, I grew up learning about different varietals and methods of making wine. My favorites tended to be the pinot noirs, so I opened up a bottle of Gate Sonoma Coast and poured two glasses. I went into the living room, where Luke was examining my record collection. I had actual vinyl records, which was unusual, but I was a collector. I was old-fashioned that way. Not that I didn't love my digital collection, too, but there was still something about having a vinyl record that was something that just couldn't really be duplicated.

He was smiling, as I gave him the glass of wine and he continued to thumb through the collection. I had everything in there from Sinatra to hard core rap. He picked up one of my Kid Cudi albums with interest. "Man on the Moon," he said. "Nice. I would have never pictured you as a Kid Cudi fan, but it works." And then he chuckled as he also saw that I had everything that Eminem and Drake had put out on vinyl as well.

I smiled back. "Songs of my youth," I explained. "I'm kinda old school that way. But I'm not totally uncouth in my musical tastes. Notice that I also have quite a few classical and jazz records in there as well."

He nodded his head, smiling big. "I did notice," he said. "Gotta love a woman who can appreciate both Mozart and some good old fashioned rap as well." He continued to thumb through my Green Day and Weezer collection, pausing to also admire my Adele and Amy Winehouse records. "Boy, you are old school," he teased. "You got anything made in the last ten years? Not that being old school is a bad thing, though."

I went over to where he was, and started flipping through to my more current records. "As you see, everything is arranged by genre and approximate era. You just didn't go far enough."

He nudged me playfully with his leg as he continued to flip through and admire my collection. "Guess you're right," he said, as he picked up individual records and admired them.

I examined him while he had his nose in the liner notes of the record he was looking at. I couldn't tell if he was genuinely interested in my record collection, or if he was nervous and didn't really know what to say. Which would have been unusual, as he had no problem talking to me earlier at lunch. Our conversation then was easy, unforced and flowing. Now he just seemed a bit tongue-tied, and I wondered how I would loosen him up.

Sad to say, my first instinct was to try to make some kind of sexual advance. It was then that I realized just how far I had gone with my random hookups. Like I couldn't relate to men on any other level than that. And it was also, right at that very moment, that I had the epiphany that my behavior up until that point had been rather shameful. I made a silent vow to change.

"Well," Luke finally said. "Why don't we put some of these records on and play a game or something? I'm assuming that you got some cards around here somewhere, don't you?"

"I do," I said, as I took the vinyl records that were in his hands and lined them up on my console. Then my door buzzer went off, and I went to it and buzzed up the delivery guy. A few minutes later, I was bringing the food into the house. I got a couple of plates, and spooned the food onto them, and brought it into the living room. Luke and I dug into our food with gusto.

The first record dropped, *Bedtime for Democracy* by the Dead Kennedys, a band that was popular well before I was born. An interesting choice, considering we were settling down to play some cards and perhaps try to get to know one another better, but a good choice all the same. Also on tap was Frank Sinatra's *September of my Years*, Adele's *21*, *Under the Pink* by Tori Amos and Weezer's *Red Album*. All amazingly old school, most of them from well before I was born, but all pretty much classic by my standards. I wondered if we would get through all the A sides of these records before he left, and found myself wanting that very much.

As the music played in the background, Luke and I got into some card playing and chatted a bit while we ate our food. "So," Luke said. "I hope you don't mind the fact that I read that *Time* magazine article about your life." He seemed shy and apprehensive as he brought this up to me.

"Not at all," I said, as I dealt the cards. "How about some *Phase 10*?" I asked him, referring to the progressive card game that took several hours to play. It was always one of my favorite card games, having learned it from my maternal grandmother Charlene. We used to play it for hours when she visited, and I really looked forward to those evenings when I was very small. "You know that game, right?" I asked, taking it for granted that he did. I assumed that everybody knew that game, as everybody probably had a grandmother like mine.

"No, actually, I don't," he said.

"Okay, then, I'll teach you." I then explained all the rules of the game. About how each hand was different, and each hand got progressively more challenging. I explained about how to keep track of points, and how it was best to have a low score, rather than a high one, and how different cards left in his hand when I would go out meant varying amounts of points. He listened intently and got it rather quickly.

"Sounds fun," he said, "let's go."

I dealt the cards, and asked "okay, go on. You saw the article in *Time* magazine about me. What did you think?"

"I think that you're art is absolutely in-fucking-credible," he said. "And, I hope you don't mind my saying, but it's an absolute tragedy that you have taken such a long sabbatical."

I pondered his words, considering the fact that he didn't come right out and say that I had quit, but, rather, carefully chose his words in saying "sabbatical." I liked that he said that, because it did make me consider my long break in a different way. I was on a sabbatical, like a professor, as opposed to having given up. "Thanks," I said, "I appreciate that."

He looked at me some more, his beautiful eyes sizing me up. He took his cards, and looked them over, and then looked back at me. "No, Dalilah, I'm serious here. You have a phenomenal talent, and I know what I'm talking about.

I've studied all the masters, just like you, and I know a once-in-a-generation talent, and you definitely are that."

I felt just a little bit uncomfortable at his fawning. Deep down, I kind of knew that he was right. I was talented, I did have something unique, and I did throw it all away. I needed to work on my confidence again, and, truth be told, Luke was actually helping in that department. Still, I wasn't good with compliments. "Uh, thanks. Now, let me pick up some cards and discard some."

I saw him visibly get just a little bit frustrated, and then he shrugged his shoulders. He picked up some more cards himself and discarded some more, and then announced that he had the necessary hand to lay it down.

Eh, beginner's luck. I transferred some more cards, but, before I knew it, he had gone completely out and I was stuck with all the cards in my hand. I sighed, and counted up the cards "Well, this game is getting off the ground wonderfully for me," I said sarcastically.

He smiled his goofy smile, his dimples broadening on his cheeks. "Card shark, huh?"

I didn't want to tell him that I was, actually, a card shark when I really wanted to be. I had mastered the art of card counting, not that it would have mattered much in this game. "Beginner's luck. Don't get too cocky," I said teasingly.

But, the next few hands went the same way. Luke was really starting to take to the game, and I didn't mind that he was. I wasn't overly competitive, really, and was happy to see that he was winning.

"So, Dalilah," he said, casually laying down yet another hand. "I can't help but wonder what happened. I hope that I'm not prying."

"It's like this, Luke," I said, finally being able to lay

down a hand of my own. "I was a young child when I was getting all of this attention. I was just 10 years old. I suppose you also read in this article that I have a very high level of, well, smarts." I hated to talk about myself in this way. It always sounded so pretentious and obnoxious. Yet, I had to discuss the issues.

"Yes," he said. "Your overall level of intellect is astounding to me, to say the very least."

"Well," I said. "What nobody tells you about prodigies and geniuses is that our emotional maturity is virtually the same as anybody else our age. So, it's very difficult to be advanced. Critics certainly didn't understand this. They saw my work, and just assumed that, because I had the skill set of an adult, I also had the maturity of one." I shrugged. "Not so much. I was absolutely devastated by the avalanche of crap that came at me after that Jacobs article. I couldn't function after a little while. My father tried to hide all these magazines and articles from me, but, of course, I had the Internet, so I was relentless in seeing what the critics were saying about me. It was all so glowing until that Jacobs article, and then they suddenly turned on me *en masse.* And I know it might be difficult to understand, but I started to lose my identity and my inner core. I was virtually silenced by my own critical voice."

"Okay," he said. "How can we bring that back?"

"I don't know," I said, honestly. "I guess that I just need to become fearless again. I wish that I knew how to do that."

The next record dropped, and the card game continued. We talked a bit more about what was going on with me, and I commented about how much I loved his work as well.

"Let's just form a mutual admiration society," he said with a smile. "I think that we are completely enamored with each other's work. Perhaps we could be each other's cheer-leaders. I can help you get back into it, and you can help me not lose hope that I need to just go back to Maine and become a fisherman like my dad."

I was startled at such a suggestion. "You can't become a fisherman," I said. "I mean, not that being a fisherman isn't a noble profession. It is, of course. But you have too much talent to do anything else but art."

He smiled, and blushed. "Well, your words and about $7 can get me a nice cup of Starbucks coffee. But thanks."

I dealt the cards. "What about Nottingham? He sees your talent. He hired you, after all, to paint me."

Luke shrugged. "Well, I might as well come clean right now. I got that job because of a sketch I made of you."

"Of me? I don't understand."

He looked uncomfortable. "Please don't think that I'm a stalker. But I saw you on the bus. I was on my way to see about a commission, so I was in the city. And you got on the bus. And, well, you lit up the entire city. So cliché, I know, and I'm sorry. But that was the only way that I could describe you. You just looked incandescent. I couldn't take my eyes off of you."

I felt myself blush, which was a different reaction for me than was usual. I mean, I had heard men talk like this to me before, but I had never heard such words delivered with such passion.

I didn't say anything, but just stared at my cards. My hands were shaking, and I actually felt tears forming. Why I was about to cry was a mystery to me. I only knew that I was moved by what he was saying.

So he went on. "So, anyhow, I had a really shitty evening that night. I came home to see that I had been robbed, again, and I needed something to cheer me up. I immediately saw your face in my mind again, and I, well, sketched you from memory."

I was becoming overwhelmed at his words. He was obviously infatuated with me, somehow, from the moment he saw me. Like my father was with my mother. And something inside me was screaming that I virtually felt the same way about him when I first met him. Perhaps I wasn't acknowledging as much, that I felt a thunderbolt when I met him. But his words were bringing these feelings to the surface, and they felt more than a little bit uncomfortable. Mainly because these feelings I was having for him were still so alien for me.

So, instead of acknowledging to him how I was feeling, I made a little joke. "You weren't robbed," I said. "You were burglarized."

"Come again?"

"Well, lots of people get these two terms confused. A robbery only happens when something is forcibly taken from somebody else. Like a when a little old lady gets her purse snatched. That would be a robbery. But when somebody breaks into your home and takes stuff, that's a burglary. It's a different thing. Kinda like the difference between jail and prison. Those are other terms that people always get confused."

"Oh, okay," he said. "Thanks for the criminal justice 101 lecture." He grinned, but I could tell that he was a bit nonplussed that I hadn't addressed the evidence of his infatuation-at-first-sight.

My hands were still shaking, and I swallowed hard. It was difficult enough for me to be feeling this way about Luke, but to put my feelings into words seemed impossible. I hoped that I didn't quite scare him away with exterior coldness. Inside, I was feeling completely warm and fuzzy about all that he was saying to me. It was just a shame that I couldn't outwardly express how I was feeling on the inside.

He was carefully studying me as he laid down some cards. "Dalilah, I think that you're looking a bit red in the face. Perhaps you're allergic to this wine." He genuinely looked concerned about this prospect.

"No, uh, no. I'm not allergic. I'm just, uh, feeling rather…"

It was then that he suddenly, and without warning, put down his cards and planted a soft kiss on my lips. I inadvertently lost my breath, as I bit his upper lip just a little bit. The tingles that I was feeling at the diner became magnified times 1,000, it seemed. This feeling was like nothing that I had ever in my life experienced. His lips were warm and he smelled of caramel for some reason. He put his hands on the sides of my face as I wrapped my arms around the back of his neck and brought him closer into me. He put his hand on my waist as he hungrily seemed to devour me with his lips and tongue. He was an amazing, passionate kisser, and he seemed to put every ounce of his being into it.

He laid down on top of me, his rather nice hard-on poking through his jeans. But, then he blinked rapidly, and suddenly stopped.

I looked at him quizzically, wanting, more than anything in this world, for him to continue. Usually when I was with a guy, I simply wanted the whole thing to be over with. Nottingham was the exception, but that was only because I was so intrigued with the sex games. But, usually, I could care less about the men that I had been with.

But with Luke…I felt that I just didn't want him to continue, I *needed* him to continue. My body was crying out for more of his kisses and was crying out for him to strip off my clothes and make love to me. Every cell in my body seemed to be screaming for him to continue. I also realized that I had been breathing extremely heavily.

He kissed me again for several more minutes, gently yet forcefully. He then lightly brought my wrist up to his mouth, and he nibbled on it. This, too, brought shudders to parts of my body that I had never even thought about before.

Then, just like that, he stopped again. He shook his head. "So sorry, Dailah. I don't know what got into me. That won't happen again."

NO! He obviously didn't know that my body, and my mind for once, was begging him to continue. Craving for him to continue. I blinked my eyes, and tried mightily to catch my breath. I was a runner – I tried to jog about four miles a day to stay in shape, which, of course, seemed to be contradictory to my other unhealthy habits, namely my drinking – yet I was feeling my heart race as I had never felt before. And this feeling like I was underwater and couldn't breathe – that was something that had NEVER happened to me before.

After a few minutes, I finally recovered enough to speak. "That's fine, Luke. I mean, I liked it. I mean, I want that to happen again." I was talking like a moron, I was well aware of this. Yet my thoughts were scattered and jumbled and I couldn't tell which way was up anymore.

His face was completely red, and he just shook his head. "You're my muse. Perhaps that's all you should ever be."

"If I'm your muse, then you shouldn't keep me at arm's length. You should envelope me in your strong arms and make me feel like you just did." I put my hand on his leg, and I lightly kissed his cheek, but that was all that I did. For some reason, it just didn't feel appropriate to be aggressive with him. I wanted him to continue to make the moves on me. I was feeling shy, which was another alien feeling for me.

This Luke was suddenly making me feel different on so many levels. It was all very foreign and strange for me, yet wonderful.

Luke cracked his crooked grin and put his arm around me. "Oh, Dalilah?" he said, softly. "How did I just make you feel?"

"When you kissed me, I don't know how to explain it. It was like I came alive. That's the only way to say it. I have been so numb for so long that I have forgotten how to have authentic feelings. But I'm suddenly starting to remember."

Then, to my utter dismay and chagrin, I started crying.

Luke was alarmed. "Dalilah, what is it? Why are you crying?" He put his strong arm around me, and put his hand in my hair. I could hear his breathing, strong and regular. His heart was also audible in my ears. Boom, boom, boom.

I shook my head. "I don't know. I just realized that I've been numb for nine years. I had such passion when I was very young for so many different things. I was able to translate all of those strong feelings onto the canvas. But when I lost my voice, I lost myself. My passion and feelings. Gone. But when you kissed me…"

I swallowed hard. He was still looking at me, his goofy grin gone. Instead, he had a look of concern in those gorgeous eyes. "Go on, Dalilah," he whispered.

I shook my head. "I remembered. I remembered what it felt like to actually want something. To actually care about something. Isn't that crazy? It was like something was actually triggered in me when you kissed me. It was like a flashback. A flashback of how I used to be."

I also wanted to explain to him that I was feeling regret,

too. Regret for how I was wasting away. I had everything given to me at birth, and I chose to throw it all away because my feelings were hurt. I was feeling more than a little bit silly, too, for making excuses for my absurd lack of motivation over these past nine years. If I knew somebody like me, I would want to strangle her. Slap her to try to wake her up. Tell her to quit whining and get with it.

And explain to her how to be fearless again.

Luke was still looking at me with those eyes of his. I was feeling more than a little bit mesmerized by them right at that moment. He stroked my cheek gently and said "it's not crazy at all. Sometimes it just happens that way. Something small and insignificant will catch your attention, and, just like that, you're spun back into the past. It happens to me all the time."

I wanted to tell him that his kiss wasn't "small and insignificant" to me at all. That it was everything. But I somehow didn't have the words to express these thoughts. So, I just nodded my head, and silently willed him to continue.

But, he didn't. The mood seemed to be broken with him, much to my dismay, because he started getting up off the floor and said "well, Dalilah, I'm going to refresh my drink, if you don't mind. I see that you're empty too. Do you mind if I refill yours as well?"

"Sure, Luke, that would be great." My heart was still racing, as I had yet to recover from the overwhelming feeling I had when he kissed me. I looked down at my hands, which were shaking, still.

Who was this Luke Roberts, and why did he have the ability to shake me to my core? When nothing, and nobody, else ever has had the same ability?

He refilled the two wine glasses and sat back down next

to me. "Okay, then, where were we? I think that we were on the seventh hand. Remind me again what we're looking for here?" he said, as he shuffled the cards.

"Um, two sets of four," I said. "Looks like this might be a long hand," I said, looking at my cards, which were nowhere near forming the two sets of four that I would need to lay them down.

"Two sets of four," he said, looking at his own hand and motioning to me to set down some cards and pick others up off the pile. He furrowed his brow, his grin and dimples back on his face. He shook his head and laughed a little bit, which I was already picking up to be his "tell" that he didn't have a very good hand.

"So, Luke," I said, as the game went on. "What kinds of things do you think about when you get some kind of trigger? You were just talking about how little things spin you into the past."

He shrugged. "Sometimes I miss the old man. I mean, he's still alive, and living in Portland, Maine. Still just as crusty as ever. But I don't necessarily see him as often as I would like, and there are times when I genuinely miss him. So something small might remind me of him, and I get nostalgic for stuff. For the days when he was my pop, and I was his little tyke, and we spent long days trying to catch fish in the river. He was an expert, of course, but he always wanted me to be the one to bring home the prize catch."

I listened to him, charmed already at his story. "Go on," I said, not wanting to interject with my own stories of my youth, which is what I would usually try to do in such a situation. Instead of listening to the story, I had a bad habit of interrupting with my own stories, but I didn't want to do that here.

He shrugged again. "Eh, anyhow, he had this organ that

he bought one time. My mom thought it was the silliest goddamned thing in the world. But my pop loved it. He played it all the time. But he got tired of it, and eventually it started gathering dust, so he gave it away. But, you know what? I came across an organ just like it in the Salvation Army one time, and it really triggered strong emotions in me. Silly, insignificant, but that organ really took me back."

I took a deep breath. "How is your relationship with him now?"

"Strained. He thinks that I'm wasting my life out here. Thinks that I need to get a real man's job, like he has. Sometimes I think that he might be right about that."

That startled me, to say the least. "Why do you say that?"

"Well," he said, finally laying down his hand. "Sometimes you just have to admit defeat and set aside your dreams for a better life. There are too many starving artists in this city as it is. I don't want to be one of them for too much longer."

Suddenly, I started feeling anxious. It sounded like he might not be in the city for much longer. And, for some reason, just imagining that he might leave town was something that was inconceivable to me, and would be devastating.

"I don't think that giving up on your dreams would ever qualify as having a better life," I said. "You might make more money doing something else, that's true. But true happiness comes from following your passion."

"I know. But true happiness also comes from not getting stuff stolen all the time, and having something to eat that doesn't come from a box labeled *Ramen Noodles*." He smiled and laughed a little. "Not that this describes me. I've got bars on my windows to keep out the burglars. Not the robbers, but the burglars. So, hopefully the problem with getting stuff stolen won't be for too much longer."

I didn't know what to say to that. What I did know was that he was wickedly talented, and just needed the right break to come his way. He was still quite young, too. He just hadn't had the time to make a name for himself.

I also had to admit to myself that I had no idea what he was going through, as far as his fear of abject poverty. I was privileged, I knew this. Yeah, I was also stubborn, therefore I steadfastly refused for my mom and dad to give me any money at all. No matter how much they begged me to take it. But, at the same time, I also had to admit that they were a safety net. It would take a lot for me to swallow my pride and ask them to support me, but, if it came to that, I could do that. Luke, on the other hand, didn't appear to have the same safety net. So, I didn't know where he was coming from. I really didn't have the fear, as he apparently did, of facing living on the streets if things didn't work out.

Then he smiled again. "I'm just kidding. I'm doing okay. I wasn't until Nottingham came along, and, well, now I'm doing alright for at least a little while. Ah, but when that well runs dry..." He shrugged again, and started to deal the cards. "Guess I just have to live on my bartending tips for awhile."

I looked at him, wondering what to say. And also realizing that I was feeling a great deal of electricity just being that near him. His faint scent of *Dolce and Gabbana* cologne, with its hints of rosemary and cardamom, was making my heart race. I was staring longingly at his chest, which was covered in a sweater, yet I could see the faint outline of the hard muscle underneath. And the memory of how I felt when his lips were on mine...there were no words to describe that.

He was sitting there so casually, too, his knee up, with his left arm dangling from it, holding his cards. Even the fact that he was left-handed made me turned on, because I subconsciously associated lefties with intelligence and creativity. Mainly because my father, and Nick, two of the most intelligent and creative men I had ever known, both were lefties.

As was I.

I bit my lip, wanting to attack him, but restraining myself from doing so. "You don't have to live on your bartending tips," I said, perhaps too quickly. My wheels started turning, and, to my utter dismay, turned to Nottingham.

Nottingham, who Alaina told me owns "more than a few galleries." He apparently was a patron of the arts. How much of a patron, I knew not, as I hadn't yet dug into researching the man. I apparently had Nottingham wrapped around my finger, though, for whatever reason. His constant phone calls and texts to me after our encounter told me this. Might I be able to subtly persuade him to give Luke a platform for his work?

Or would that be too risky? After all, I was feeling very strongly for Luke. It wasn't simply that I was wildly attracted to him, more than I had ever, and I mean ever, been to any other boy or man before. But I also was feeling a strong emotional and intellectual connection with him. His art spoke to me on a visceral level, which spoke volumes about his depth as a person. I was so anxious to get to know him on these deeper levels.

And Nottingham was infatuated, if not obsessed, with me. He might not take too kindly to me promoting Luke to him, especially if he would be able to tell exactly how I felt about Luke.

It certainly would be threading the needle, trying to get Nottingham to be Luke's benefactor, without Nottingham knowing exactly the reason why I would want this. I couldn't just come right out and tell Nottingham, obviously, that I was falling in love with this magnetic man Luke. That wouldn't be good at all, to say the very least.

I would have to think about this one. I would obviously have to be deceptive to Nottingham to get what I really wanted here, and deceit was never something that had come naturally to me. Too bad I didn't have more of Alaina in me.

I vaguely became aware that Luke was staring at me. "Dalilah," he said. "It's your deal."

"Oh, yes, sorry," I said. I couldn't concentrate, though. My mind was whirling with how to help Luke find his audience, which would come, I knew, if he could get a few showings. And, truth be told, my mind was also whirling with thoughts that were not so pure. Specifically, I was thinking about how much I really wanted to see what was underneath that sweater and jeans he wore.

I cleared my throat and started to deal some more cards. My hands started shaking again, and I said "you know, it's getting really warm in here, isn't it? I have no idea why. I don't have the heater up all that high, and the atmosphere outside certainly isn't warm." It being October, the night air outside was hovering in the low 50s, and I knew that I hadn't cranked my ancient old-school heater high enough to make the room feel as muggy as it was feeling to me right at that moment.

But Luke apparently was also feeling warm. "You know, I didn't want to say anything, but I know what you mean. I hope you don't mind if I take off this sweater."

"Not at all," I said, trying to ignore the inner voice that

was screaming *take off your button down too! In fact, take off those jeans and everything else!!!!!*

He took off his sweater, and he was now just in his white button-down, which had the top two buttons unbuttoned. I could see his sculpted muscles now, which were peeking out under his shirt, and I also could see more of the outline of his hard chest and abs. His strong arms were also more on display.

I took a deep breath, trying very hard to tamp down the feeling that I was getting, which was that I wanted to rip off that shirt with my teeth. Instead, I tried to concentrate on his hands, which were gripping the cards. But even that failed to quell the burning sensation that I was feeling, because his hands were as sexy as the rest of him. They were strong, yet delicate, with well-kept nails and long narrow fingers. It struck me that they were artist's hands. Don't know why that thought occurred to me, but that was what popped into my head at that point.

And then he put his cards down, and his beautiful hand was on my cheek again, and his lips were on mine once more. This time the kiss was soft, feathery and light. I closed my eyes, wanting to drink him in. Wanting to devour him, and for him to make me want to scream out in pure ecstasy. I had never yet had an orgasm, except for the orgasm that I had with Nottingham's sex games, and that one didn't really count. Because it wasn't an orgasm that was healthy. It was just an orgasm that happened because I was woken up.

But, with Luke, I knew, I just knew, that he could bring me to orgasm in a more tender and healthy way. In fact, I was feeling something like an orgasm happening already, just with him kissing me. I was becoming flushed and warm, and my body was radiating with pleasure.

My heart was pounding again, but Luke pulled away.

"Dalilah, it's getting late," he said, as my heart absolutely sunk into my shoes. "I have to pull a double shift at the bar tomorrow, so I need my rest. And I'm sure you need your rest, too. But I'll be seeing you tomorrow morning for your sitting?"

I nodded my head silently. I attempted a smile, but I wasn't sure if I pulled it off.

He smiled and got his sweater and put it on his arm. "I'm sorry we didn't finish the game," he said. "Next time, huh?"

"Next time," I said, praying that there would be a next time. "We left off on the eighth phase, so just two more to go, and you're well ahead," I said, glancing at the score sheet. Indeed, he was smoking me on points.

He tousled my hair a little bit. "I'm sure you're letting me win." And then he leaned down and kissed me again. "Good night, Dalilah. Sweet dreams."

"Sweet dreams," I said, as he opened the door and let himself out.

And, just like that, he was gone.

But I didn't go to bed after he left. In fact, I stayed up all night.

I stayed up all night painting, my fingers furiously digging into my watercolor set, the brush stroking across my canvas.

I had never in my life felt so goddamned alive.

Chapter Fourteen

Luke

As I made my way down Dalilah's stairs, and into the cool night air, I thought about how I could never tell Dalilah why I had to leave so abruptly just now. It was that I felt that I couldn't breathe, yet I had a raging hard-on that quite frankly embarrassed me. I knew for a fact that I had never quite had a hard-on like the one I had in her apartment. She was quite discreet in not looking at my crotch, thank god, because if she did, she definitely would have seen it. Because it was tent-like in its proportions.

So, I had to go to the diner that was just down the street, and hit the bathroom the first thing. Two minutes later, I emerged, feeling much more in control of the situation.

And, of course, I had to buy something there, because using a diner's restroom without buying anything was just plain rude. So, I sat down at the corner booth and ordered a cup of coffee. As I sipped the coffee, I pondered the evening.

I felt excited as I realized that Dalilah was definitely feeling something for me. It was in her words and in her body language. She wanted me as much as I wanted her. That much was perfectly clear.

But it just wasn't as simple as all of that. I wished that it would be. But it wasn't. I couldn't give her what she needed. At that moment, I just wasn't able to give any woman what she would need. I wasn't established. Dalilah deserved somebody who could monetarily afford to treat her like the platinum that she was. Yeah, Nottingham was allegedly going to be giving me $5000, but the contract stipulated that it was to be paid after the project was over. I had just noticed that the other day when I was reading the fine print. So, in the meantime, I was broke.

And Dalilah was like a bottle of *Domaine de la Romanee-Conti Grand Cru, Cote de Nuits*, which was recognized as the finest wine in the world. She was unique, rare and well out of my league. That I was increasingly feeling that I was falling for her, and I was feeling that more and more, every time I saw her, was a non-factor. I simply couldn't have someone like her, and that was that. As frustrating as that was.

I doodled on the napkin in front of me, and then, just like that, song lyrics started pouring out of my head. That wasn't something that usually happened for me, because inspiration for my lyrics constantly eluded me. But being up there with Dalilah - feeling her warmth, seeing her extraordinary beauty, and sensing her even-more-extraordinary intelligence – somehow did inspire me as nothing else ever had.

So, for the next hour, the lyrics poured out of me. What

came out was a sappy love song like the kind that I used to make fun of when I heard it on the radio. With the exception of The Beatles *Something* of course – there was no arguing with that classic. But, usually, when I heard a love song, I rolled my eyes. Because there wasn't such a thing as the kind of pure love that these songs conveyed.

Or so I thought. But I was increasingly seeing a glimpse, but just a glimpse, of what these songs were talking about when I looked into Dalilah's eyes.

I finally decided to walk to the subway station, which was a few blocks away from her apartment, around 3 AM. I did have a double-shift at the bar the next day, which was going to kill me, I knew. I was going to be dead-tired. And Dalilah would be coming to my studio at 8 AM, too. For that, I knew that I would be wide awake.

I tried very hard to tamp down the feeling of absolute excitement that was bubbling up as I anticipated seeing her again in just a few more hours. For she was still untouchable to me in so many ways. I was amazed that I had the nerve to kiss her, but, then again, that was how I was feeling about her. I couldn't not kiss her. I couldn't not fantasize about making love to her. I had such an absolute passion for her that touching her and kissing her almost seemed like it was second nature to me.

But my brain said that what had happened up there with her – the kisses – was going to be as far as it ever could go. She was my muse, of that I was sure. She inspired me to write a rather kick-ass love song, if I do say so myself, and she also inspired my art. I was finding myself increasingly incorporating her, in some way, in everything that I was composing, even if it was as an abstraction of some sort. Like I would be painting a picture of people in a café, and there she was, popping up at one of the tables. Or I was doodling a sketch of a busy city street, and Dalilah was there in the crowd.

And, of course, there was the portrait of Dalilah that I was creating for that wealthy bastard, a portrait that I was suddenly feeling proprietary over. Which was a dangerous way for me to feel, because I didn't own this portrait. Nottingham did. I was just the instrumentality for getting the portrait done. Just the same, the entire project was turning into one that was a passion project for me, moreso than anything else had ever been. How I wished that I could keep it for myself after it was finished!

Yes, she was my muse. And she might always be, even in the near future when I would inevitably be forced to jettison my art and make it just a hobby, while I found a "real" job that would pay the bills. She was my muse, but she could never be my lover. I hated to think that I just wasn't worthy of her, but that was what went through my head.

I might have been falling in love with her, but I still couldn't imagine being with her.

Nonetheless, I looked forward to seeing her again with breathless anticipation.

Chapter Fifteen

Dalilah

After Luke left, and after I had feverishly completed my first painting in 9 long years, which was not something that was in my previous chosen genre of urban expressionism, but was, rather, a simple and straightforward realistic portrait of Luke himself – hey, it was a start – I found that I simply couldn't sleep. I was too anxious to get down to Queens and see Luke again at 8 in the morning.

I tossed and turned and tossed and turned. I knew one thing for sure – he had awakened in me something that was powerful and couldn't quite be put into words. It wasn't just sexual, although, I had to admit, that was a really big part of it. I wanted him, sexually, more than I had ever wanted anybody. In.my.life. But, no, what he awakened in me was a burning passion. It was as if these past nine years, where I went through life in a kind of twilight fashion, didn't even exist. There was color in my world again, so much more than there ever was.

I saw a movie once, long ago, when I was a very young child. It was kind of an old movie, even then, but it was called *Limitless*. Some of the movie was in grey, drab tones – that was the part of the movie that showed how the protagonist was seeing the world during that period. But he took some kind of magic pill that caused him to use 100% of his brain, and, at that moment, the world suddenly had color. Lots of bright color.

That was how it was with me. Suddenly, I felt like being engaged in the world again. I was seeing things again that made me want to take to my canvas, and put aside the fear that I had been carrying around with me for so long. To finally just say to hell with the haters, I was going to paint what was in my heart. There were going to be haters, I knew that. There always were. But I couldn't listen to them. I had to go with my own muse and my own instincts and get right back to it.

And to think that this newfound passion came from just one kiss...

Nope, it wasn't just the kiss. It was the feeling that Luke gave me. The feelings that were inside me all along, but were dormant, suddenly felt like they were about to burst forth and overwhelm me. I suddenly realized that all that I really needed in this world, which perhaps I never realized before, was the feeling of being in love. As crazy as that was, thinking that I was in love with this magnificent boy after just a few hours of talking with him and feeling his soft lips on mine, that was just what had happened.

My mind raced forward, and I knew that I also had to keep Luke in town, somehow, someway. He was struggling with his art. Why he was, I didn't know. No, I did know. He was just like everybody else was who was wildly talented and penniless. He needed a platform, a way to introduce his artistic talent to the world. He had to have a way for every-body - art critics, art patrons and the masses alike – to know exactly how gifted he really was.

I wished that I knew somebody who was in that world. Who ran in that circle. I certainly used to. I knew all the great artists back in the day. The critics, too, and the patrons. I might have only been 11 when I was getting my recognition, but I could intellectually engage with anybody, so talking to artistic types was never a problem for me. But I had long since fallen out of that world.

Yes, I was modeling for established artists, none of whom had the kind of reach that I needed. I really needed somebody who had money to be Luke's benefactor, and also somebody who had powerful and monied connections. The *right* powerful and monied connections.

I knew that I, myself, would soon be back in that world, and, if things went the way that they went before, I would presumably be getting showings again. I could sense that, even though I no longer would have the draw of curiosity that I had before as a prodigy. Galleries did want to work with me back then, in part because I had such a name due to my status as prodigy. I no longer had that status, of course, as I was 20 years old, therefore nothing necessarily set me apart from others who were in my field. So, I might have to start small with my own showings, which didn't necessarily help Luke any.

No, I had to figure out a way for him to shine.

Tapping my fingers on my desk, I got up and Googled Nottingham. For the next three hours, I found out every-thing I could about him. And there was one thing that was inescapable to me. Nottingham had just the profile I needed to help Luke out. He was extraordinarily wealthy – as Alaina had said, Nottingham owned many different things in lower Manhattan. He also owned no less than 10 different galleries around the city, many of them working with well-established international artists. He was a silent partner in about 20 others.

Somebody like him could make or break an artist in this city, I thought to myself. And he also had some powerful friends who were well-known in the art circles. I found this out as well in my exhaustive research. I had no idea if Nottingham himself was artistically inclined – there was nothing in my research that would indicate that was the case – but he was certainly a patron and benefactor of the arts. And he had exquisite taste in who he chose to bestow his considerable largesse.

Chapter Sixteen

So, I knew what I had to do with Nottingham and with Luke. I was very anxious to begin my plan, though, so I was admittedly distracted when I saw Luke for our posing session. I was bubbling over with enthusiasm and excitement, and it seemed as if these particular emotions were larger than life for me. I guess because I had spent so many years of my life being tamped down and muted – my emotions were, at least – that now that the dam had finally been broken open, it was like fireworks were bursting in my head. As silly as that sounded, that was what life was starting to feel like.

I went to his studio, meeting him there right on time, of course. I felt incredibly shy to be sitting there in front of him, stark naked. Another very odd emotion for me - I never felt that way before when I posed for him. Now, however, it didn't seem right that I would be naked for him. It seemed premature, like I shouldn't have him see me nude until it came time for us to actually make love. Of course, I couldn't exactly express any of this to him. He had a job to do, as did I, and both of us would have to carry it out with the utmost of professionalism until the project was finished. And that was that.

For his part, it seemed that he, too, seemed a little bit embarrassed to be painting me. He blushed even more profusely than usual, and he seemed a little bit tongue-tied.

"Okay, Dalilah," he said when I arrived the studio. "Uh, go ahead, and uh, you know…" As he was talking, he was pointing at the divider in the room, and not meeting my eyes. He was looking down at the floor, and his hand was shaking a tiny bit. He noticed his own hand shaking, because he looked at me apologetically and said "don't worry about that. My hand will be rock steady when I take to the canvas, I promise. I don't know what's wrong with me this morning."

I knew exactly what was wrong with him, though, even if he didn't acknowledge it. He had feelings for me too, strong ones. I could feel it. So it just wasn't natural for us anymore to be merely artist and subject. He was feeling that, I knew.

And, when I emerged from behind the divider, I could feel my own face blush hot crimson. I felt so completely self-conscious, I felt like screaming. But I kept my cool, as much as possible. So, I laid there, just like normal, on the fainting couch, trying very hard not to concentrate on what was happening - that Luke was seeing me naked before he really should have.

Another thing that was going through my mind was that I wanted Luke to make love to me very badly. I really, really did. For the first time in my life, I wanted to be made love to, which felt absolutely wonderful. But I also knew that I didn't want that to happen for a long time with him. I wanted to get to know him, body and soul, before we made love. Which was another reason why I didn't really want to be naked in front of him anymore. There was just too much sexual tension now. It could be cut just like a knife. It was exceedingly difficult for me to be there, because I was feeling aroused like I had never before felt. It was actually physically painful, being that aroused and not being able to do anything about it. And I could just imagine how he was feeling. It was probably even worse for him.

That was when I realized that he was wearing baggy pants. Much baggier than usual. And I suddenly knew why. He was no doubt as aroused as I was, but he had to hide that fact, so he had to wear baggy pants. I thought about how I had gotten a glimpse at his erection last night when he had come over. It was quite nice and quite large. There was no hiding it in the fitted jeans that he was wearing. So he had evidently thought about that angle ahead of time, and had decided to wear pants that would hide his excitement.

The thought of that made me smile.

He smiled back, as he sat behind his canvas, concentrating fully. His eyes twinkled and his dimples were back. "What's that smile about, Dalilah?" he asked me, his left hand furiously working on the canvas.

I shrugged my shoulders. "I was just thinking about last night," I said. That was partially true. I *was* thinking about the previous night, in the context of remembering his erection when he kissed me.

He blushed again, and shook his head. "Yeah, I'm sorry about that, Dalilah. I don't know what got into me, kissing you like that. That wasn't very gentlemanly of me."

"No, no, no, Luke. Please don't apologize for that. I liked it. I mean, I really, really, really enjoyed it."

"I'm glad," he said. "But, really, you can do better than

a starving artist. So, I really had no business being as forward as I was last night."

I took a deep breath, realizing that there was going to be some complications in pursuing what I really wanted in this situation. Which was an honest-to-god relationship with him. A relationship that was just like what my parents had. My parents, god love them, were as crazy about each other as they had ever been. I realized when I was an infant that mom and dad were nuts about each other, because I understood, even then, about emotions and love. And, as I grew up, and I watched them, I knew that what they had was special. More special than anything else I had ever seen. None of my friends had parents who were as deeply in love as mine.

Both of my parents were, individually, crazy in their way. But put their individually crazy personalities together, and, somehow, someway, it was pure kismet for them. Serendipity. Fate. Whatever word you want to use to describe two people who really got each other, and knew just how to make the other person happy, that would be the word that I would use for them. If I was at all spiritual, which I wasn't, I would use the words "soul mates." But that all seemed silly to me. I didn't believe in the concepts of heaven, hell or souls. But if there was such a thing as a soul, then my parents would be considered to be each other's soul mates.

And that was really what I was searching for. A relationship like my parents'. I could somehow see that Luke had the potential to give this to me. He couldn't see it. He was evidently too blinded by his own sense of inadequacy. Not that I could blame him - he knew about me. About my family's wealth. About my own background as a prodigy. That would be intimidating to many, if not most, men.

Which gave me even more resolve to try to help Luke behind the scenes. Luke just needed to have confidence in his own abilities, and he also needed to have financial security. When he had both of those things - which would come, I knew, because I had so much belief in his artistic abilities – then he would feel worthy of me.

In the meantime, though, I knew that there was very little that I could say or do that would convince him that he was worthy of me right at that very moment. He was a man, and, as such, he had to feel that he could provide for me, or for any woman that he would be with. I knew enough about the male gender to know how Luke was feeling, and there wasn't much that I could do to dissuade him from feeling that way.

So, I just decided to bide my time with him. "Okay, Luke," I said. "I understand. But I want to be friends with you. In fact, I would love it if you would meet my parents. They're moving here soon. In fact, they already have a home in Montauk, and they're in the process of actually getting the movers to get them out here. I kinda promised them that I would see them once a month. So, when I do see them, I would love it if you could come with me. You and my dad would really get on very well. He's an artist, too, and he's really brilliant."

Luke blushed again. "I know about your dad. God, you probably think that I'm a total stalker now."

I was curious about that. I didn't remember there being any big article about my father, except for the *People* article all those years ago. I wondered if Luke had taken the time to actually research my father as well.

"I don't think that you're a stalker," I said with a laugh. "What do you know about my father?"

"Well, I became really interested in you and your background when I Googled you," he said. "So I wanted to find out all that I could. And Googling your father was quite easy. I'm so sorry. I feel like I invaded your privacy. I just didn't want you to explain to me about your family and your father, when I already know about them."

"Don't worry about that," I said. "It's not a secret or anything. My father lived for years as a drug addict, as you know, and he also had a male lover. Which you also know." I watched Luke's face, which showed no surprise, so it was obvious that he had found the *People* article. And he probably also found the other articles, more recent ones, that talked about my father's animal rights foundation and animal sanctuary.

He nodded his head. "Yes. I mean, I also found all those other articles that talk about the good work that he's doing right now with those animals. That's really amazing. He seems to have such a huge heart. Your mother, too, because I know that she's also involved with the charities." Luke seemed anxious to not dwell on the negatives, which I appreciated.

"Yes," I said. "My father has boundless compassion, and my mother as well. They're tireless in their charitable contributions to the animals. They both have such a passion for it. But I'm sure that you also know that my mother also had her problems when she was young. That was all in that *People* article as well."

Luke nodded his head. "Yes, I know. I have known many people like your mother. Cutters. It's sad that she had to go through all of that, but she really overcame it very well, too, from all that I read about her life now. Your parents are really remarkable people, and I would love nothing more than to meet them. If you really want me to." He seemed shy again when he said that last part. As if he was afraid that I was somehow only inviting him to meet my parents because I wanted to be polite.

"Of course I do," I said. "You'll love them. They might be billionaires, but, really, you would be hard-pressed to meet two people who are as down to earth as they are." I paused for a moment, thinking about them. And then, it was as if I had realized something for the very first time. I was lucky to have them as parents. I was lucky to have grown up surrounded by their guidance and love.

To my surprise, I felt a tear come down my cheek.

Luke looked very concerned when he saw me cry. "What is it, Dalilah?" he asked. He got up and handed me a box of Kleenex, and I blew my nose as more tears flowed down my cheeks.

I shook my head. "I haven't been a very appreciative daughter. They've tried so hard to reach me for so long, and I have just ignored them and really made them feel like I don't care about them and what they have to say. That was so wrong of me. A girl really couldn't ask for better parents than them." I felt so guilty, as I realized that I just had yet another epiphany. It was so weird – now that I was actually feeling emotions again, everything was starting to bother me. My behavior, in general, was bothering me. The sleeping around, the drinking in excess, the bitchiness to my parents – all of this was suddenly making me feel very, very ashamed of myself.

Luke put his strong arm around me, and I put my head on his chest while I cried. He had a chest made of steel, and his skin felt very warm. I sat there, feeling sad for my behavior, yet also feeling that I didn't want to move. I loved the feeling of my head being in contact with his chest, even if I still had to feel his pecs through his clothes. I longed, so much, for him to be shirtless, with my head on his chest. I wanted, so much, to run my fingers on his naked body. To take my tongue and trace it around every inch and crevice of his no-doubt beautiful form.

My heart started racing, as I realized that my tears had dried, and I also realized that my overwhelming feelings of guilt were now replaced with overwhelming feelings of pure lust. Unadulterated lust. All I could think about was how I wanted Luke to be as naked as I was at that moment, and how much I wanted the two of us to spend the entire day on this fainting couch just leisurely exploring each other's bodies with our fingers and our tongues.

But Luke was still comforting me. He apparently didn't know that I was feeling so much heat and excitement just being so close to him, because he was sympathetically stroking my hair and talking softly to me. "There, there, Dalilah. I'm sure that your parents know that you love them. But if you are feeling badly, you really need to give them a call and tell them how you are feeling. And you are so very lucky to be able to actually call them and tell them that you love them. I wish that I had that option with my mom."

And, just like that, I was jolted back into reality. Luke apparently had lost his mother. I felt so badly for him at that point in time.

I looked into his eyes. "Oh, Luke, I'm so sorry. How did you lose your mother?"

He shook his head. "That's not important," he said. "I'm sorry. I guess that just slipped out."

I looked at him, and put my hand on his cheek. "I'm listening," I said. "I would love it if you could confide in me. I mean, you know all about my family. I'd love to know more about yours."

He just shook his head. "I'm so sorry, Dalilah. I'm sorry.

But it's still very raw for me. I mean, it shouldn't be. It's been ten years since it has happened. But I haven't been able to talk about it with anybody." And, at that, he got up and went back to his canvas. "Anyhow, where were we? I think that I need to get about another half hour in, and then we can quit for the day."

I felt disappointed, not only because Luke apparently was hiding something about his mother, but also because Luke was no longer holding me in his arms. I wanted to simply melt in his arms, like a block of butter, and, now that he was back behind his canvas, I suddenly felt very cold and alone.

"Uh, I guess I was still posing for you, and you were still painting me."

He smiled and nodded his head. "Yes, that's just where we were. This portrait is really coming along nicely. Nottingham should love it. At least, that's the idea. God forbid he thinks that it sucks." But then he shrugged his shoulders. "Ah, the worst that could happen is that he says it sucks and he refuses to pay me. Then I would have this portrait for myself to keep. That would hardly be punishment."

I cocked my head at him. "It wouldn't be punishment? Why do you say that?"

"Because then I could always have this beautiful portrait of you. So, when you and I are done with this project, and you inevitably forget about me and find the wealthy guy who can treat you like the precious and rare diamond that you are, I will always have something that will remind me of you."

I suddenly felt overwhelmingly sad for Luke. Sad that he couldn't see what was in front of his face – that I wanted to be with him. I knew that. He evidently didn't. I also felt sad that he thought that being treated like a cold jewel was something that I ever wanted out of a relationship. I wanted somebody who would treat me like the flawed person that I really was. Not somebody who held me up on a pedestal.

Luke evidently did have me on a pedestal, and that was incredibly frustrating for me. I knew why he put me on the pedestal, though, of course. He evidently couldn't see me as clearly as I would have liked. He seemed to be blinded by his own insecurities in that regard.

I got up off my sofa, and went over to him. I didn't look at the portrait he was making, of course. I never wanted to see these portraits until they were finished, and this was no exception. But I carefully went over to him and held out my hand for him to take.

He tentatively put his hand in mine, and looked at me questioningly.

I took a deep breath. "Okay, Luke. I'm going to say this only once. You can either believe it or not. I can't convince you if you already have your mind made up about this. But I will tell you that I'm crazy about you. I've thought of little else but being with you, ever since you came over last night. I know that it's sudden, because we don't really know one another all that well yet. But I feel that I'm falling in love with you."

Luke's beautiful eyes got wide when I said that, and his entire face broke out into an enormous smile. But he also flushed a deep scarlet. He gripped my hand tightly in his own, and then he looked down at the floor. He still didn't say anything, though.

So, I continued. "Who knows? Maybe I am my father's daughter after all. He fell in love with my mom at first sight. She thought he was crazy, or at least that was how they told it to me. So, we Gallaghers are known for falling for people pretty quickly. I never thought that it would happen for me like that, until you kissed me last night. And then I knew."

He looked like he might start to actually believe me. But, then he shook his head. "Oh, my god. I don't know what to say. Except that I'm feeling the exact same way about you, Dalilah. I didn't think that it would be possible that you would feel the same way about me." His voice trailed off, and he looked at the wall, which was reflecting the light from the window. "Never thought it was possible."

And then he took his hand away from mine and he gripped his paint brush tightly with both hands. He stared at the brush for a few minutes. He shook his head again and looked at me. My heart stopped as his beautiful eyes, which looked blue in this light, met mine. He put his hand on my cheek. "Oh, Dalilah, how I wish that things were different. How I wish that I would be able to give you the world. But I can't possibly ask a woman like you to be with a boy who has bars on his windows to keep out the burglars. That's the reality of the situation."

I put my hands on the back of his head. "I know, Luke. I know how you are feeling. But I also know how I am feeling. And I know, as sure as I am standing here, that you're going to be able to give me the world, if that is what you want. You are far too talented to live the rest of your life in poverty. Believe me. I wouldn't say this if it weren't true. I don't blow smoke up anybody's ass." And then I smiled. "No matter how cute that ass happens to be in a pair of jeans. Anyhow, I digress."

He smiled, too, at my little joke. But he looked down at the floor again. "Yeah, talented people never die in poverty. Like Van Gogh, Poe, Franz Schubert and Vermeer."

I put my hand on his chin. "Hey," I said. "Don't dwell on those giants. Think more about Picasso, Warhol, Arbus,

Ansel Adams, and any number of artists who became rich and famous during their lifetimes. That's going to be you. You're not going to fit the stereotype of the penniless genius. I completely believe in you. Now, you just have to also believe in yourself."

He smiled and took my hands. "I know, Dalilah. I know that I'm talented. I just don't have the certainty that you apparently do that the rest of the world is going to find out about my talent. Because, so far, I've just been drowning because I'm just one talented artist in an endless sea of others who are just as talented."

I smiled back, because I *did* have the certainty that Luke would be discovered, sooner rather than later. As long as I could manipulate Nottingham to do what I wanted, then Luke would have the platform to show himself to the world. And the rest would fall into place.

Of course, Luke had no way of knowing the devious plan that I had in my head. And there was no way that I would ever tell him about it. He would think that I was crazy.

"Well, Luke, let's just say that I know that you're going to be discovered. There's no way that you won't be. In the meantime, just know that I want to be with you. I would be with you right now, bars on your windows and all. I can't convince you of this, of course, but I want to put that out there all the same. I just want you. But, since you apparently feel that you have to be successful before we can be together, then the only thing that I can do is bide my time until that happens. And I will, Luke. You have opened up my eyes and made me feel things that I didn't think that I was capable of feeling. So, there is no way that I am going to let that go."

Luke took a deep breath, and held my hands. "I wish that I really believed that, Dalilah." He paused, and then looked at me. "Because I think that I'm already in love with you."

I smiled, and felt my entire body flushing all over as he said that. I felt like jumping up and down with joy, just knowing that Luke felt that way about me.

"I'm in love with you, too, Luke. And we will be together. You can be sure of that."

He stood up and stroked my cheek. "I wish that I could be sure of that, Dalilah. Believe me, I wish that I could be sure of that."

I looked at him and thought to myself *you will be sure of that. When you become a world-renowned artist, thanks to Nottingham giving you major showings, you will be sure of the fact that you and I will be together.*

Of course, the consequences of manipulating Nottingham like that was far, far from my mind at that time. I only knew what was right in front of me. Looking back, I wish that I would have thought everything through just a little bit more.

Chapter Seventeen

I left Luke's studio, reluctantly, after my session. He apparently had to pull a double-shift at the bar, so he had to leave, and I had to admit that, as I sat on the bus bound for home, I really was missing him. I was starting to feel that I wanted to be with him all the time. I almost hated that feeling, though. I certainly didn't want to be clingy and needy.

But Luke had also made me realize how desperately lonely I was. The loneliness was palpable suddenly. I never really had thought about it in quite that way. I always thought that I wasn't lonely, I was just bored. After all, I was independent and always had been. I never really thought that I needed close connections in my life. Now, for the first time, I was realizing how wrong that was. I was lonely, desperately lonely.

I tried not to think about that when I got back to my apartment. Then I started to think about using that lonely feeling as inspiration for my next work. Which I did, as I conceived of a barren landscape in a post-dystopian world. I was going to get my feet wet with my art again.

I worked for several hours, watching the clock to see when I could contact Nottingham. I knew that he was at work, and, truth be told, I really didn't know his hours. But I figured that it might be safe to call him in the late afternoon.

After several hours, I stood back and looked at my work. I cocked my head, and tried to silence the critical voice in my head that said *it's terrible, Dalilah. You're a hack. You're not good and you will never be good again.* I had long since lost confidence in my own ability to evaluate my work, so I really didn't know if what I had painted was good or not. What I did know was that it was definitely a start. And it really did express how I was feeling. Lonely, alienated, disjointed, removed from the world. I was coming back from being like that, because of Luke. But, at the same time, Luke was keeping his distance, so there was still the feeling in my mind of hopelessness and despair.

Finally, I got to a stopping point and took an enormous breath and called Nottingham's private line. He immediately picked up.

"Dalilah," he said. "Took you long enough to respond to my entreaties."

I groaned inwardly. Who used the word "entreaty" in regular conversation? Pompous asses who want to show off their SAT vocabulary, that's who. Nottingham turned my stomach. *I'm doing this for you, Luke. You will never know that I did this, but you will get the benefits of it.*

"Yes, Blake," I purred. "I'm so sorry. I got really busy. Anyhow, I'm calling you now. I know that you want to see me, so I thought that perhaps we could get together soon."

"I knew that you would, Dalilah. The other night has been on my mind constantly. You were so game. I really would like to do that on a regular basis. I think that you will find that I can be a most interesting and stimulating lover."

Oh, boy. How was I going to get around this? "Blake, let's talk about that later. Right now, I just thought that we could meet for a drink or something."

"Meet me at the Union Club. Tonight. 7 PM. Do not be late."

And, just like that, he hung up.

The Union Club. I had never heard of that place. I was thinking that he and I would meet at some bar. I had no idea if this place was a restaurant or bar or whatever.

So, I Googled it. And, of course, it wasn't a bar or a restaurant. It was an exclusive rich guy's club, the most exclusive in the entire city. I read that this club was so exclusive that even the sons of the most prominent members were denied admission. This club was known for its opulence, five dining rooms, lounge, and humidor with 100,000 cigars. Members have included Cornelius Vanderbilt, Dwight D. Eisenhower, William Randolph Hearst and Ulysses Grant.

I groaned, wondering how I was ever going to get into this place. I would imagine that Nottingham would arrange to meet me outside the place so that he could get me in as his guest. I had visions of the movie *Titanic*, where the rich assholes sat around drinking brandy around a fire and discussing politics and other dry topics, while the peasants down below were having the time of their lives.

Yup. Luke was my Jack Dawson, while Nottingham was definitely Cal Hockley. I giggled as I suddenly realized this. But then again, it wasn't really all that funny, as Cal got pretty stalky and murderous in that movie when he realized that Rose and Jack had fallen in love. Nottingham definitely had that potential as well. I could see that.

I definitely wasn't looking forward to this meeting. I would have to put him off when he would inevitably suggest going back to his place for more fun and games. I was going to have to walk a fine line between teasing him enough to think that he still had a chance with me, and actually going to bed with him again. I had no idea how I was going to thread that needle, and I also knew that one false move would have the opposite effect of what I wanted. Nottingham had the potential to make Luke in this town. He also had the potential to break him even more.

And Luke couldn't be broken down further. He and I were really a lot alike in one respect – we both had little confidence in our own artistic abilities. I was astounded to realize that this was still true with me – that I thought of myself as a hack as I stared at what I painted on my canvas. I never thought that before, when I was young. I guess because I had so much outside encouragement and adoration that I knew that I was good. Now, it was only me who was looking at my own art, and I just didn't trust my inner voice and my instincts on this. I wasn't fearless anymore.

And Luke. Well, he probably did know that he was talented. He had to. But he hadn't exactly gotten the positive feedback that would be necessary for him to really know his own potential. And, if things didn't go well with Nottingham, then the danger would be that Luke might have an even more difficult time getting noticed, and this would further drain his confidence. And if Luke never found his own confidence, than there really was no hope for my relationship with him.

So, the stakes of my meeting with Nottingham were uncomfortably high.

I questioned myself as I sat on my hardwood floor, my back against my hide-a-bed. The bottle of whiskey was staring at me, beckoning me, but I ignored that siren call. I started breathing heavily as I anticipated all that might go wrong. But I couldn't think of any other way of getting Luke a platform in this town. I was at an absolute loss. Nick was wealthy and had lived in this city for a long time, but, as far as I knew, he didn't know any large art patrons. My father was wealthy, but he hadn't even moved to the city, so he didn't know any large benefactors either.

Finally, I just decided that I needed to talk to somebody with a devious and subtle mind. A mind that I definitely didn't possess.

I went down to Alaina's and knocked on her door.

Chapter Eighteen

Alaina answered the door. "Dalilah, what a nice surprise!" she said, as she stepped aside for me to go into her place. "Twice in one week. To what do I owe this pleasure?"

"Wow, you're in a great mood," I observed. She did look happier than usual. "Are you busy?"

"Later, yeah. I mean, I should be studying, but you know how that is. Oh, wait, you don't. You never had to crack a book in your life." She was smiling as she said this, so I assumed that she wasn't meaning to get in her usual digs about my brilliance and how it was so unfair that I never had to study.

"I hope that I'm not keeping you," I said tentatively.

She smiled broadly. "You're not. But if you are wondering why I am looking so happy and fulfilled, I'll let you in on it. I'm dating your sloppy seconds, Seth, and boy, you're an idiot for giving him up. That boy puts me on another planet in bed."

I shrugged, feeling no jealousy about Alaina dating Seth. I was happy for her, though. "Cool," I said. "Well, enjoy. He's hot and has a huge package, and he does tend to be insatiable. So you'll no doubt enjoy the ride, no pun intended."

"Oh, I am enjoying the ride. I am. Six times last night I enjoyed the ride." She shook her head. "Man, Dalilah, I have no idea what you were thinking when you blew him off. But, at the same time, it really sucks, because he's still so in love with you that you're all he talks about. When he's not fucking me, that is. Of course, I'm waiting for him to start calling me Dalilah in bed, and then I don't know what I'm going to do."

She shrugged her shoulders. "I really hope it doesn't come down to him wanting me to put on a red wig and role play being you. But, it might. Anyhow, what's up?"

I took a deep breath. "Well, you remember Nottingham? BDSM man?"

"Yeah," she said. "You aren't going to see him anymore, right? Right?"

I was silent for a few minutes, and Alaina got the drift.

"Oh, fuck, no, Dalilah. You can't be with a weirdo like that who gets off on beating you. He really needs to be with a submissive masochist who enjoys that stuff. I would like to think that isn't you."

"It's not," I assured her. "It's not. Well, I need to come clean with the whole sorry story about why I'm going to go out with Nottingham. I need your advice."

So, I told her everything. About how I had fallen in love with Luke, and how Luke had no confidence and didn't feel that he could be with me because he couldn't provide for me. And how Luke felt that I was out of his league. How I thought that Nottingham could help Luke, and how I hoped that it would all lead to Luke and I being together.

Alaina digested it as I spoke to her. Finally, after I told

her the whole story she nodded her head. "Well, let me get this out of the way. I'm shocked that you fell in love. Shocked. I didn't think that it was possible. Good god, every hot guy in school was in love with you and you just didn't want any of them. Now, here is this dirt-poor boy and he's the one you want. It figures."

"Why does it figure?"

"Well, you can't have him. So, naturally you want him."

"Now, come on. That's not why I fell in love with Luke. I just, well, he brings out the best in me. My best self. Emotions that I never thought that I could feel. He makes me want to be a better person. He has opened my eyes. I can't possibly give him up now."

"Well, then, you shouldn't have to. But I know what you're saying about him not wanting to be with you because he's poor. Men are like that, just by their very nature. It's evolution. They're supposed to be able to provide for us and take care of us, and, since he can't do that, I think that you're right that he won't want to be with you."

"I know that I'm right about that. So, what do you think about my Nottingham plan?"

She put her chin on her palm and stared at her coffee table. Finally she said "I don't know, Dalilah. It's risky. How, exactly, are you going to manipulate him without sleeping with him again? And you can't just see him and say 'hey, I don't want to be with you. But I really want you to help out this Luke fella.' That won't go over at all."

"I know that," I said, feeling impatient. "That's why I'm down here talking to you. I mean, you have a devious mind, much more than me. How am I going to work this? Nottingham is no dummy, of course."

"Well, Dalilah, you're going to have to start fucking him again. On a regular basis. And, when you guys have been fucking for awhile, then you can start talking to him about Luke."

"Thanks, Alaina," I said, rolling my eyes. "You've been an enormous help."

"What, do you want me to lie to you? Nottingham isn't stupid, and I doubt that he can be manipulated to give you what you want without you first giving him what he wants. So, don't even think about it."

I started to despair. If Alaina, the queen of manipulation and games, couldn't think of a good strategy, then who could?

"Okay, then, I guess I'll just have to try what I can, and, if it goes south, I need to just drop it with him." As much as I didn't want to do that. Luke needed Nottingham's largesse. I knew that.

I could feel my relationship with Luke start to slip through my fingers.

Finally, Alaina sighed. "This Luke means this much to you, huh?"

"You have no idea."

"Well, then, try this. You obviously don't want to sleep with Nottingham. I don't blame you there. The man seems dangerous, and, besides, if you're in love with this Luke boy then, of course, you don't want to sleep with somebody else. You can, however, date Nottingham without sleeping with him."

"I can? How do I do that?"

"You say that you have the herp. And, if he gets angry with you because you slept with him before, just tell him that you didn't know that you had it then. Tell him that you're really contagious right now because you're in the middle of an outbreak."

I stifled a feeling of laughter that was threatening to

break out. The plan seemed too simple. And, of course, there was always the threat that Nottingham might just decide to drop me altogether once I tell him that I have herpes. Which would probably mean that he wouldn't exactly want to help Luke on my behalf.

I shook my head. "That's sounds good, but no. I would imagine that Nottingham would probably want nothing to do with me after that, which would mean that he wouldn't want to help Luke if I ask him. I don't know, he seems kind of germaphobic as it is. He probably wouldn't want to touch me with a ten foot pole."

She shrugged her shoulders. "Well, Plan B is that you tell him that you have turned over a new leaf and you don't want to fuck until marriage. You've been revirginated."

I looked at Alaina, pondering her words. *Now, that just might work out well.* I thought about Nottingham and the things that he had said to me. About me being a lady, and how I should act more proper. Nottingham was so buttoned-up himself that I was surprised that he had sex with anybody, let alone that he was a freak in bed. Telling Nottingham no sex until marriage would actually be something that would work.

I started to get excited, knowing that I might be able to date Nottingham and get him to fall in love with me. And then I could start putting the bug in his ear about Luke's talent, and how much I would like Luke to get prominent showings. Then, once Luke was established, I could dump Nottingham and marry Luke.

Perfect! What could possibly go wrong with that plan?

I went over to Alaina and hugged her. And she put my head in her hands, and kissed me gently on the lips. I pulled away, not wanting that to go any further.

"Oh, sorry, Dalilah. Man, sometimes you make me want

to be a lipstick lesbian. What is it about you that attracts everyone you meet like bees to honey?"

"I wish I knew," I said. "Anyhow, Alaina, I have had fun with you in that way. But you know that I'm really straight. I think you are, too, but I know that you want to experiment. And, really, go for it. Just not with me."

She shrugged again. "Guess I'm really horny. So, you have to go so that I can call my fuck-puppet Shane. I want to climb him like a tree, just like I did last night."

"K. Well, thanks for the fabo idea. I'll let you know how it goes."

"I hope you know what you're doing. At any rate, good luck. But don't be surprised if the manipulated becomes the manipulator, and you get in over your head with this one. If that happens, don't say that I didn't warn you."

"Noted," I said. "Well, I'll head back to my place. See you soon."

"Bye."

And, at that, I left to go and get ready for my date with Nottingham.

Chapter Nineteen

I made my way to the bus to go and meet Nottingham, having borrowed something else from Alaina that would be presentable for this fancy rich man's club. I had on a pencil skirt in grey and a silk top in black, a grey cardigan that matched the skirt, with black pumps and pearls. I even wore hose, for the very first time in my life.

And…Nottingham was waiting for me on the sidewalk. He got out of a limo that was parked in front of my apartment as I approached the street. I inwardly groaned and rolled my eyes. *Of course he would be here. Why did you ever think differently?*

He opened the door and kissed me on the cheek. "Dalilah, you look stunning," he said. "Absolutely a vision."

I smiled as I stepped into his limo. The seats were cool and some soft jazz was playing on the stereo.

Nottingham got into his side and he directed the limo driver to the Union Club. "Get us to the Union Club on 69th and Park," he said. The limo driver nodded his head, and Nottingham turned his attention to me. He put his arm around me and whispered "my god, you are a beautiful woman. I think that you are, by far, the most beautiful woman that I have ever seen in my life."

At that, he turned my head and planted a firm kiss on my lips. I held my breath, wanting the kiss to end as quickly as possible. I couldn't stop thinking about Luke. I felt guilty and dirty even to be kissing somebody else.

Nottingham grabbed my thigh and his hand started up towards my panties. I quickly and rapidly pushed it away. He looked at me questioningly, and, for once, he didn't look cruel or lustful. He just looked bewildered.

"I'm very sorry, Blake," I said. I had practiced what I would say to him in the apartment, but I didn't know that I would have to give him my speech quite this soon. I thought that I could say it when we got to the club, where I could have a glass of wine and tell him in a more leisurely and relaxed fashion. But no, it had to happen there in the limo, while Nottingham was trying to crawl all over me. "There's something that I need to tell you."

"Go ahead Dalilah," he said.

"Well, here's the thing. I've decided that I've been a bad girl and I want to clean up my act. I've done a lot of thinking, and I'm ashamed of how I have behaved. So, I decided that I need to stop having sex outside of marriage. I hope that this isn't a problem."

He smiled. "Not at all," he said. "I was hoping that you would actually say something like this. You're a lady. I'm so happy that you are finally realizing that. So, don't worry. You can wait until we get married. And then I can ravage you like you have never before been ravaged."

I drew a breath. That was really easy, I thought. He was delusional, of course, thinking that he and I would ever be married. It was strange that he was even thinking along those lines, considered he barely knew me. Also, well, he was extremely desirable, in that he was extraordinarily handsome and wealthy. I really had no idea why he would want to try to get married so soon, especially to a woman who had made it somewhat clear that she didn't love him. At least, I hoped that it was clear that I wasn't really interested in him that way.

The limo finally pulled up to the provincial French building on Park Ave. This was an enormous stone structure that apparently was constructed in 1863. Which was obvious as we went through the doors, where there were two marble staircases and a huge insignia on the floor that said "1863" in gold letters against a black backdrop.

All around us were well-heeled men and women who were heading into the main restaurant. I felt uncomfortable, not because I didn't fit in, of course. Because, my parents being billionaires, I certainly did belong there. But that kind of place was just never my scene. Joey's dive restaurant in Willets Point – now that was a place where I could feel comfortable. This place, not so much.

Nottingham took my hand as he led me into the main restaurant. This was an enormous dining room with chandeliers and wood-covered walls. It was very opulently appointed, with crystal glasses and candles on every table. The maître d' sat us, calling Nottingham by name. We sat down, and I looked around me. Everywhere were tycoons and their well-heeled wives. The men all looked very old money, and their wives were elegantly dressed and tended to have helmet hair. I felt a little bit underdressed, even though I knew that I looked good. But my gown wasn't beaded nor formal, and most of these people were in their charity-ball clothing.

The waiter came around, and Nottingham ordered for

both of us, not even bothering to first ask what it was that I wanted. We both were going to get the braised squab with *Chateau Chalon* sauce and *au jus*, served with whipped potatoes and asparagus. While that did sound good – I had squab before, and it was tender and delicious – I was quite put off that he would order for me without even asking me what I wanted.

A bottle of wine came out, a vintage *Le Pin*, which retailed for over $2,500, and was selling there for $5,000. The waiter poured the wine for Nottingham and me, and then left. Nottingham raised his glass to mine, and we clinked the glasses together. "To a wonderful life together," he said, and took a sip.

I said nothing. This was getting weirder and weirder by the second. It occurred to me that this man might have created an entire relationship between the two of us in his head, long before he even started making his presence to me known on the sidewalk bench that day.

I took a deep breath. "This is a beautiful place," I said, stating the obvious.

"That it is," he said. "So, Dalilah, I can't tell you how happy you have made me to finally decide to give our relationship a chance. I've been dreaming about this for years now."

I took a sip of wine, feeling more than a little bit freaked out. I questioned my sanity in deciding to go out with this guy. What was I thinking? He was a stalker, and I knew this to begin with. I was blinded by my desire to help Luke.

That was when I remembered exactly why I was there with Nottingham. To help Luke. This thought calmed me down.

"Well, Blake, I couldn't stay away," I said, trying for my best throaty, sexy voice.

"I've thought of nothing but you since the other night. You were so magnificent and so adventurous. I admit, in the limo, I was a bit non-plussed to know that our sexual adventures will have to cease for now. But just wait until we're married. We definitely will make up for lost time."

Time to steer the conversation onto more safe territory. "Yes. Well, Blake, I must say that you have definitely hired a very talented artist to portray me. I think that you'll be thrilled with the results." I cocked my head. "By the way, I was wondering if you had looked at Luke's website yet? He really is an exquisite talent."

Nottingham nodded. "Yes, of course I have looked at his website. I admit, I hired him on the spot without checking his credentials, just because he had sketched an amazing likeness of you. But I did some research on him later on that evening. The boy is clearly very talented. I'm very glad that he is the artist that I have hired. I think that he'll do a wonderful job."

This is going to be quite possibly easier than I thought. I wondered if Nottingham was as naïve I was thinking. I mean, the man was clearly intelligent, but that didn't mean that he didn't have a blind spot. And he seemed not to pick up on the fact that I was touting Luke to him for a reason.

Feeling more confident, I pressed forward. I put my hand on Nottingham's arm and stroked it while I looked into his eyes. His blue eyes, which looked hopeful, met my gaze. I started to feel bad, because Nottingham was beginning to show real emotion. He no longer had a cold and cruel look, but was actually looking just a bit…human.

"So, anyhow. I've been doing some thinking. Luke has this extraordinary collection of urban alienation landscapes. They're really quite remarkable. They're very thematic as well. I thought that they just might be perfect for a showing in one of your galleries."

Nottingham put his hand to his chin, and looked at me thoughtfully. "You know, I was thinking the same thing." He shrugged, and then regarded his glass of wine. "I was looking at his website, and I saw that most of his paintings were thematic. I personally favored his panels on musicians and ballerinas, and I thought about talking to some of my partners about featuring them in one of our upcoming shows that center around that very theme."

My heart started to race. This was going to be easier than I thought! It was! I smiled big. And decided to drop the entire subject. I didn't want Nottingham to get even a hint of how I was really feeling about Luke, and I thought that, if I kept talking about Luke, I might let on. And that would, no doubt, put a kibosh on the entire thing.

"Well, that's a really good thing. I'm glad that you want to give that boy a chance. Anyhow, how are things with you?"

He took a sip of his wine. "Things are really splendid. It's going to be a very good year for Nottingham Industries. Very profitable. And, of course, I'm very happy that you are here with me." He paused. "You have no idea what you do to me, Dalilah. I know that I have seemed like a stalker to you, and perhaps I am. I don't want to think of myself that way, though. But you are just...glorious. I think that's the word that I want to use to describe you. Glorious. I can't stop thinking about you."

Uh, oh. He was really gushing now, and, to my dismay, he actually looked sincere when he was speaking. It wasn't like the other night, when he had a cruel look on his face and it seemed that he just got off on hurting me. Right at that moment, he looked vulnerable and a little bit lost. I started to feel sorry for him, and feel sorry that I ever went out with him just to manipulate him.

Not that I wanted to be with him. No, that wasn't it at all. I still had no feelings for his man, and still very much wanted to be with Luke. Luke was all that I could think about. But I never thought that I would start to feel sympathy for Nottingham, which was exactly what was happening right at that moment.

I opened my mouth to say something, when, to my dismay, Nick and Scotty came over to our table. "Dalilah," Nick said to me. "I thought that was you."

I was startled, and I jumped just a little bit when I heard Nick's unmistakable baritone address me. Scotty looked beautiful, as usual. She had just turned 40, I realized with a start, but she hadn't aged since I had first met her when I was three years old. I hoped to look that good when I was 40 and had three children with Luke.

I smiled as I realized that envisioning children with Luke came as easily to me as breathing. That was when I realized that I truly was in love.

And Nick...well, men just get better with age, and he was no exception. He had just turned 50, and, even though he had a few grey hairs, he was fit and trim and had barely a line on his face. He was like Dorian Grays – ageless and still beautiful. I wondered if he had a portrait of himself somewhere hidden away that was aging as we speak, while he, himself, stayed just as youthful as ever. I had just a slight crush on him when I lived at his house, because he was so handsome, intelligent and virile. Just a school girl crush, which was typical, really.

I smiled, big. "Hi, Nick," I said. And then I turned to Nottingham, who was regarding Nick warily. When I looked at Nick's face, I saw the reason for Nottingham's wary look, for Nick was giving him the stink eye. Unmistakably.

It occurred to me that, even though the two men knew one another, they probably didn't really like each other. I didn't know what Nick knew about Nottingham, but I had a feeling that whatever it was that he had heard wasn't good.

Nick nodded his head. "I heard your dad's going to be in town soon." He said those words not just to me, but to Nottingham. As if he were warning him.

"Yes, he is," I said. "I think that they're going to be moving into that Montauk house next weekend."

"Good," he said. "I think that he needs to keep an eye on you."

At that, Scotty kind of nudged Nick, and then she smiled at Nottingham as if to reassure him that Nick wasn't meaning to impugn him. She extended her hand to him. "Blake, I'm so sorry that my husband hasn't acknowledged you. But it's so good to see you."

Nottingham stood up and nodded his head and shook her hand, and kissed it gently. "As always, Mrs. O'Hara."

Nick nodded to him without bothering to shake his hand or even say his name out loud. "Well, Scotty and I have to go. We were on our way to the Met." He raised an eyebrow at me, and didn't acknowledge Nottingham. "I'll be in touch soon," he said, and I thought that perhaps his words sounded just a bit ominous.

Scotty came around and bent down and kissed my cheek. "It's so good to see you, Dalilah." And Nottingham stood up again and kissed her hand again. "Always a pleasure, Blake," she said.

"The pleasure is all mine, of course," Nottingham said.

At that, the two of them headed towards the exit. Nottingham sat down and took a drink of wine.

I tentatively asked. "What was that all about?" referring to the tension between him and Nick.

He shrugged. "I don't think I know what you are talking about."

"Nick. You and he seem not to like one another."

He tried to look genuinely surprised that I would say something like that, but I could tell it was all an act. He clearly knew what I was talking about. "I don't know what you are talking about. Nick and I go way back."

"Huh," I said, but said nothing more. At any rate, I knew, as sure as I was sitting there, that Nick would be calling me soon to read me the riot act about being there with Nottingham. That was one thing about Nick – he always told it just like it was. I was going to get an earful, I knew.

Nottingham and I finished our meal, and I decided to say nothing more to him about Luke. It sounded like he was on the fence, anyhow, about featuring him. I didn't want to push Luke too much on him, lest Nottingham get suspicious on why I was doing so. So, for the rest of the evening we talked about politics and other stuff upon which we didn't agree.

I was increasingly seeing that Nottingham was a corporatist who believed in little regulation. "It stifles industry, Dalilah. I think that we need to get rid of the EPA and any other regulatory agency that imposes needless and expensive regulation."

"Huh. Well, then, I guess that you haven't absorbed the lessons of Upton Sinclair. Read *The Jungle* sometime if you really want to know how corporations will behave if there isn't somebody policing them."

To this, Nottingham sat up straighter in his chair. I touched a nerve with him, that much was clear. "Don't be ridiculous, Dalilah. That was another place in another time."

"Oh? And you're telling me that corporations, who are beholden to their stock-holders and nobody else, will voluntarily be socially responsible if nobody is holding their feet to the fire? Seriously?" I snorted and took another sip of my wine. "I'm calling bullshit on that. Take away regulations, and you're going to have sweatshops making a comeback, workers toiling in unimaginable conditions, and contaminated food. Good lord, even with these regulatory agencies, we still see plants exploding right and left because they hadn't been inspected in years. Sorry, but corporations have never policed themselves, and they never will."

I was on my soap-box. Blame it on my socially conscious parents. Everything I knew about how factory farms worked, among other industries, came from them. I just hoped that he didn't get me started on anything regarding animal rights. It would be at that point that I would pour my glass of wine on his head.

As it was, Nottingham was decidedly getting angry that I was challenging him. Clearly, he was used to women who were seen but not heard. As he busily made his way through his dessert, he was glowering at me. "You really are an impetuous one. Well, that will soon change. When you're my wife, you're going to be a lady."

I took a huge breath, trying hard not to stand up and slap him and walk right out of that place. I reminded myself of why I was there in the first place – Luke. Luke was going to benefit from the sacrifice that I was making. The sacrifice being having to sit there and listen to this pompous wind-bag.

I smiled, covering up my rage. I was starting to feel sorry for him earlier, but he was back to his controlling and cold self. I never could understand men who thought that they somehow had the duty to control their woman. Make her into some kind of a Stepford Wife. Then I looked around at the helmet-heads, all of whom had impeccable manners and sat up perfectly straight in their chairs, and I was, once again, so glad that I was never really raised in this world. My wealthy parents were so far removed from this place that it wasn't funny.

Come to think of it, I was surprised that Nick was here. He must have been entertaining somebody well-heeled, because Nick wasn't stuffy or pretentious in the least.

The rest of the evening didn't go much better. In fact, it went much worse. We got into the limo, and Nottingham once again tried to finger me. I slapped his hand away, and he slapped me across the face.

"I told you no. You said that you were okay with that."

"No to sex," he said. "I want to feel you with my fingers, that's all."

"No to that, too," I said. "No to all of that."

To that, he pulled away from me and stared out the window. I evidently hurt his feelings.

Oh, well.

Chapter Twenty

I finally made it back to my apartment around 11. I knew that Luke would still be working at the bar, because he said that was going to close. So, I threw on a pair of jeans and a sweater and made my way to where he worked.

I had to see him. After being with Nottingham that evening, my depression was coming back strong. And, truth be told, I knew that he lived above that bar. So, naturally, I was hoping that I could act like I didn't want to go all the way home that night, and he would invite me to stay over. Unless, of course, he was embarrassed. But I hoped against hope that he wouldn't be.

It was a Friday night, so the bar was pretty hopping. I watched Luke behind the bar, as he feverishly poured drinks and shot them over to the patrons and then pointed at other ones. I saw some girls evidently flirting with them, and I wanted to scratch their eyes out. Didn't they know that Luke was taken?

I didn't know how I would get his attention, or even if I should. After all, I probably shouldn't distract him. So, I stood against the wall, as it was standing room only, and did my usual routine of politely rebuffing guy after guy, until finally the waitress came over and took my drink order.

"Seven and Seven, please, with a twist," I said, giving my usual drink order. After about twenty minutes, the harried waitress gave me my drink and I took it, tipping her three dollars on my seven dollar drink. That was me, though. I tried to tip well, because I knew how hard these servers worked.

As I sipped my drink, being jostled all around, and having beer spilled all over me, I watched Luke from afar. Truth be told, that was most of the reason why I was down there. Just to be close to him. To feel his presence.

I hoped that I wasn't a stalker like Nottingham was for me.

Finally, after about an hour, Luke happened to look my way. I smiled and raised my glass to him, and his entire face lit up. That was definitely encouraging for me, because I was afraid that he would think that I was about to boil his bunny or something. Not that he had a bunny.

He shook his head at me, a smile on his face, as his attention was trained on yet another patron at the bar. He got that guy's drink, and then looked at me again, a huge smile on his face. He shrugged his shoulders as he kept getting drink after drink for the people.

Finally, it seemed that he was able to take a break, because the crowd was starting to thin about 1 AM. He leaped over the bar, not bothering to go through the little door, and rushed over to me.

"Dalilah, this is probably the best surprise that I have ever had," he said, as he put his arms around me. I put my arms around him as well, feeling his hard back muscles bulging through his tight black t-shirt. "What brings you to my neck of the woods?"

"Um, I was in the neighborhood?" I said, knowing that he was going to call bullshit on that. "No, really, I just wanted to see you. I sure do hope that isn't stalkery or anything."

"Of course not. Besides, you can stalk me anytime, anywhere." Then, at that, one of the other bartenders called him back to the bar, because the patrons were starting to swarm again. "Don't go away," he said. "I mean, I have to close, so I hope you don't mind hanging around until then."

"I don't," I said. And I really didn't, although it was usually uncomfortable for me being alone in a bar. It was always so difficult keeping the wolves at bay, and tonight was certainly no exception, as one guy after another came up to hit on me. I turned them all down politely, of course.

Finally, closing time came and the drunken people were ushered out of the bar by the bouncer. The bouncer came up to me and tried to make me leave as well, but Luke leaped over the bar again and put his hand on the bouncer's arm.

"Um, she's with me," he said.

The bouncer looked at me and said "yeah, right, Luke. In your dreams."

I smiled sweetly at the bouncer. "No, really. I'm with him."

The bouncer looked over at Luke, and nodded his head, a big smile on his face. "Impressed," he said, and slapped Luke on the shoulder.

Luke looked back at me and smiled, seemingly embarrassed. "I don't know what it is with everybody refusing to believe that you might be with a guy like me." Then he shook his head and headed back behind the bar. "I gotta clean up, but I'll be ready in two shakes. I promise."

I watched him clean up, a smile on his handsome face. He seemed to be really happy that I was there, and that made me feel immensely better.

Finally, after about a half hour, he leaped from behind the bar again and said "my lady awaits. Do you have a coat and stuff?"

"Yes," I said, and I produced it, as I had thrown it over one of the chairs. "Here it is."

He helped me on with my coat and hat, and the two of us made our way outside. Light snow was just starting to fall, the first snow of the season. I could see it in the streetlights, and it was just starting to make a light dusting on the sidewalk.

"I have to say that this was the best surprise ever," he said, as he tentatively grabbed my hand. He was starting to show snowflakes on this nose and eyelashes, and I thought about how endearing that was. "Um, where would you like to go? I mean, we can find a diner around here that is open all night, I'm sure."

I took a deep breath. "Can I see your place, Luke? I'm sure it's not as bad as you are putting on."

He looked at me skeptically for a second, then said "Oh, what the hell. I mean, we can't very well stay out here in the cold for too much longer." So, he took my hand and led me into his building. We creaked up the ancient stairs that smelled of urine, and I discreetly stepped over some condoms which were carelessly thrown on some of the steps. I grossed out when I saw a pop bottle that was filled with urine, apparently, but I soldiered on.

I had to admit that I had never been exposed to such a place before. Not that it turned me off of Luke in the least, because, of course, it didn't. I was feeling so strongly about him that he could have said that he was homeless, and I would be sleeping on the streets next to him.

Finally, we got to his apartment on the fourth floor. I wondered, briefly, why he would need bars on his windows, but then I saw the fire escape and realized that would be how the burglars were able to get into his place.

He opened the door, and I had to admit that the place really was a hovel. It was a studio, like my own, but he only had a futon to sleep on, a television and a coffee table. The place was much smaller than my place, and had the same old-school radiator that I had, which hissed in the corner. He did have proper curtains, though, which heartened me somewhat. At least he didn't resort to tacking up bedsheets, as I had seen many people do. His hardwood floors were nice, although they did seem original, so they were quite worn. And the rug beneath his coffee table showed excellent taste, as it was multicolored and geometric, which is what I usually preferred as well.

I smiled, though, even as loud music started blaring from the upstairs apartment. I looked at my watch, seeing that it was 4 AM. "Night owls, huh?" I asked, pointing to the ceiling.

"You might say that," he said. He looked thoroughly embarrassed, although I wanted to tell him not to be. "Can I take your coat and offer you a drink of something? Beer, wine, whiskey, water?"

"A water would be great," I said. "God knows I need another alcoholic drink like I need a hole in my head."

He came back from his tiny kitchen, with the very old-school appliances, a drink of water in his hand for me and one for himself. We sipped it as I looked around the room. He had turned on the stereo, and light electronica music started to waft through the air, as an unfamiliar singer wailed.

"So," he said. "Here is chez Luke. Really, it's okay, you can leave screaming into the night and never come back. I really wouldn't blame you. God knows I would like to follow you, though."

I smiled, and put my hand on his leg. "Don't be ridiculous, Luke," I said. "Yeah, this place isn't exactly a Hamptons mansion, but, no matter. You're so young, and you really haven't had the chance to make your name. But I think that things are going to change."

He stroked my hair and kissed me lightly on the forehead. "I hope so. Well, if they don't, I guess it's the fishery for me. My pop called me today, and told me that he has a job waiting for me. Doesn't pay a ton, of course, and it really is getting to be grueling work. Because of overfishing, the boats have to go further and further out to catch anything worth the effort. But I have always enjoyed the sea, so it sounds like absolute adventure for me."

I quietly drank my water, trying to tamp down the rising sense of panic in my throat that was caused by Luke talking like this. It sounded like he was going to be leaving on the first plane in the morning. I bit my lip as I looked at him. I wanted him so badly to kiss me, but he just sat next to me and didn't make a move.

I wanted to tell him what Nottingham had told me. That he, too, thought that Luke was wildly talented and that he was going to talk to some of his partners about featuring him. That would definitely be just the thing to jump-start him and his career.

But, at the same time, I felt guilty even being with Nottingham earlier. I felt dirty, almost, even though Nottingham and I didn't do anything at all for me to feel guilty about. I shouldn't have been alone with him, that's all. That's all.

I was deeply disappointed when Luke finally kissed me on the forehead and said "well, it's awfully late, Dalilah. I wish that I could provide you better accommodations, but I guess that you'll have to sleep on my couch. Let me bring you a blanket and a pillow."

"Where will you sleep?" I asked him. "Here with me, if you pull out the futon?" I felt hopeful when I said that.

"I better not," he said. "I hope you don't mind if I just get another blanket and pillow and crash out here on the floor next to you."

"I feel bad, taking your sleeping accommodations just because I happened to pop by unannounced," I said. "Let me sleep on the floor."

"I won't hear of that," he said, giving me a blanket and pillow. "Good night, Dalilah. Sleep tight, and I'll see you in the morning. No, wait, it is morning. Then I will see you when we both wake up."

I smiled, and tried to hide my disappointment that he wasn't going to sleep in the bed with me.

Chapter Twenty-One

A week went by, and then two. I saw Luke every day for our sessions, and saw Nottingham a few times a week. As little as I possibly could, really, but I felt that I needed to keep that connection going. Nottingham had mentioned that he would be speaking to his partners about Luke's work, and, thus far, there was no mention of that. So, I felt that I needed to keep up with Nottingham, and, if he still didn't mention featuring Luke in one of his galleries, then I would bring up the subject once more.

In the meantime, though, my parents were moving into their place in Montauk. I was excited for them to move there, actually, because I really wanted to see them more. Plus, I was dying for Luke to meet them.

I brought this up during one of our sessions. There still was an enormous amount of sexual tension between the two of us, as I wanted to ravage him every time I saw him, and I was pretty sure that he felt the same about me. But he still kept his distance from me.

I started to think that maybe ambushing him at his bar

was a bit of a mistake, as I saw his apartment before he was really ready for me to. I knew that he was embarrassed about his living conditions. As much as I wanted to scream out loud to him about how much it didn't matter to me that he was broke, I didn't think that would do any good, so I just didn't broach the topic any more with him.

But I did manage to convince him to see my parents with me. "My parents are moving to Montauk," I said to him, as casually as I could. "They want to see me, of course. They're going to take me to dinner at Eleven Madison this Friday night. I would absolutely love it if you could come."

His face got beet red. "I'd love to meet your parents, Dalilah. Perhaps I could join up after dinner and meet you guys for a drink or something? I mean, I'm so sorry, but I don't have proper clothing for that place. I don't own a suit or anything."

Of course, dummy. Of course he doesn't have clothes for that place. "Well," I said. "You look like you probably would wear the same size clothing as my father. You're the same height and same build and everything. Maybe he could bring an extra suit for you?" I looked at him hopefully.

He seemed hesitant. "God, that is so embarrassing to ask for that. But, if it means that much to you, then, sure, sure. Your dad can bring one of his suits for me. I might even get a haircut. And, you'll find that I clean up nicely."

Inside, I was jumping for joy. Luke was going to have dinner with me and my mom and dad! I just knew that my dad was going to love him. My mom, too, but my dad especially. My father was such an amazing artist, and he was really going to get Luke, I just knew.

"Yay!" I said to Luke. "I'll call my dad immediately and tell him to bring something for you."

So, it was set for us to meet mom and dad that Friday night at the swankiest restaurant in town. I couldn't wait.

But, before I saw my parents, I had to see what Nick was wanting. He had left several messages for me to call him, messages that I had been ignoring. I knew that his next step would be to call my father, though, so I reluctantly gave him a call.

"Dalilah," he said, picking up the phone. "Thanks for finally getting back to me."

"Well, I figured that I should call you, seeing as I'm going to be seeing my dad this Friday night. I didn't want you talking to him before I could talk to you. So, what's up?"

"I'm not going to beat around the bush. You shouldn't be seeing Blake Nottingham. Ever."

"I figured that was what this phone call was about. Give me the dirty on him."

"He's a pervert. He saw you at a party that I was throwing, and started asking everybody in the party about you. You were only 17 at the time, and he was 27. I wanted to break his legs that night."

"I know about that," I said. "He told me all about that."

"And you still want to see him?"

"Yes," I simply said. "I do." I didn't want to go into it with him exactly why I wanted to see Nottingham. It wasn't his business.

"Okay, then," he said. "Listen, I'm not one to repeat gossip, but I promised your father that I would look after you as much as I could. So, I need to warn you. I heard that Nottingham was into BDSM, pretty hard-core."

I rolled my eyes. *Another revelation designed to shock, and I already know all about it.* Still, I decided to humor him. "Oh? And how to you know this?"

"A good friend at work goes to a fetish club and sees Nottingham there all the time. From what I understand, he doesn't go easy on his submissives, either. Stay away from him, Dalilah, unless you're into that. Which I would like to think that you're not."

"I'm not," I said. "Well, okay, then. I appreciate you looking after me, I really do, but I'm all grown up now and can make my own decisions. I love you, though, you know that."

"I love you too, Dalilah. Your dad would kill me, though, if he knew that I withheld pertinent information from you about somebody you are apparently dating. I know that I can't force you do to anything, but, please, Dalilah, reconsider going out with that man."

"I'll think about it," I said. "Well, if there isn't anything else…"

"No," he said. "But take care."

"You too. It was really good to run into you guys."

"Keep in touch."

"I will."

At that, we hung up.

I took a deep breath. Nick gave me no new information, of course. And, as much as I wanted to tell Nick the real reason for my dating Nottingham, I didn't. I guess I really didn't want Nick to know about that manipulative side of me. I wanted him to always see me as the good girl that I was when I was living with him.

Of course, he knew differently, because Nottingham had apparently put the bug in his ear about my drinking heavily and sleeping around. Which made me think that Nick and

Nottingham, in general, were on reasonably friendly terms. They probably were, but Nick no doubt drew the line about a guy like that dating me. It would almost be as if some guy that I cared about as a friend dated Alaina. I wouldn't be down with that, at all, because of the way Alaina ate men for breakfast. So, I could see why Nick gave Nottingham the stink-eye. I also didn't blame him for that.

So, big whoop, I thought. Nick doesn't want Nottingham dating me, and for good reason. Well, he can join the club. *I* didn't want Nottingham dating me, either. And I knew that I wouldn't be dating Nottingham for much longer. The time was going to come when I would try to oh-so-sweetly remind Nottingham that he was going to talk to his partners about featuring Luke in one of his upcoming shows, and, hopefully, that would happen.

What I didn't know was that my intervention wouldn't be necessary after all. To my surprise and delight, I soon found out that Nottingham was going to do exactly as I wanted, without my having to say another word about it.

Chapter Twenty-Two

Luke

I was increasingly falling very deeply in love with Dalilah. Much to my own chagrin and dismay. If I could, I would stay far away from her, because she represented disaster for me. Somebody that I could never really have, yet I was continually pining away for – it felt like such a fool's errand, no matter how many times she tried to tell me that she felt the same way about me as I did about her.

What was great was that she not only was inspiring my art, but she was also inspiring my songwriting. I found myself writing love song after love song, fancying myself to be the next Lennon/McCartney after all. Some were sweet ballads, others were grungy rock songs, but all were supremely inspired. Who knows? I thought. Perhaps that would be my way of making my millions.

And, if I made my millions, I would marry that girl immediately.

So, that was really the goal. Find some way to become

wealthy. Because I didn't want to be some fool who was struggling on a middle-class income even. That wouldn't do. Dalilah was used to luxury and opulence and a certain pedigree. A pedigree which I didn't yet have, but hoped to obtain one day.

Yet, I was far, far away from even a middle-class income. So, being with her was SO out of the question, at least until I could figure out a way to make my millions.

I had sent my songs to every top producer I could think of. I Googled them, and did the querying and cold-calling. No dice, of course. Songwriting was like art, really. You have to get really, really lucky to make it. You pretty much have to sacrifice a goat or something. And I didn't want to sacrifice a goat. I liked goats.

Then, one day, a call came in that changed my life.

It was the Thursday before I was due to meet Dalilah's parents. I was going crazy with nervousness. I was quite sure that the father would automatically assume that I wasn't good enough for their daughter, since I didn't even have enough money to buy my own suit. The mom, too, although I automatically felt more comfortable about meeting Dalilah's mother, as Dalilah told me that her mom grew up as broke as my family. I imagined that perhaps Dalilah's mother might have become a snob through getting wealthy, but Dalilah assured me that wasn't the case.

"You don't understand my mom," she said. "She briefly divorced my dad when she was pregnant with me. Long story. Anyhow, when she divorced him, she went to work at Whole Foods to support herself. Even though dad gave her a shit-ton of money to live off of. And that's typical of her mentality. She still thinks like her working-class parents. That's why she's so flipping cool, and also why my dad loves her. Because he's as unpretentious as she is. So, relax."

Relax. Easier said than done. I wondered how I would feel if I was a bajillionaire and some broke artist was dating my daughter. Not that Dalilah and I were dating. Crazy thing was, we were definitely in love, but I couldn't bring myself to actually say that she was my girlfriend or even that I was dating her. But, whatever we were, I didn't think that, if I were Dalilah's dad, I would be very happy about a guy like me hanging around my daughter.

But, things did get much easier for me later on that day.

I got home, and laid down on my couch, dreaming of Dalilah. It was exceedingly difficult for me to be around her, especially since she was naked in front of me every morning. She was flawless. There was no other way to put it. Perfect skin, perfectly toned, not an ounce of fat on her, and perfect breasts. I dreamed of being with her night after night, so I also dreamed of being wealthy enough to deserve her.

Then, I saw that somebody was calling. I didn't really recognize the number, but I picked it up anyhow.

"Luke Roberts," I said.

"Hello, Mr. Roberts," a vaguely familiar voice greeted me. "This is Blake Nottingham."

"Oh, yes, of course. You probably are checking on the progress of the Dalilah portrait. It's coming along well. You may see it if you like, but you'll have to come to my apartment."

"I'm quite sure that it is satisfactory. And, no, I don't usually like to see my commissioned work before it's completed. That's not why I was calling."

"Oh, sorry," I said, feeling intimidated. This guy was so

brusque and abrupt in his speech. He perpetually sounded pissed-off, which he probably was.

"I'm a partner in the Matthew Jane Gallery in Chelsea. I trust you've heard of it?"

Matthew Jane? Of course I had heard of it. That was one of the best galleries in the city, and it worked with established artists from all over the globe. There were four Matthew Jane galleries in the city, and one that just opened up in LA. So, yeah, I wouldn't consider myself an artist if I had never heard of that gallery.

"Yes, of course," I said, still feeling mystified on why he was calling me. He surely wasn't calling me to invite me to have a showing there. That would be like some struggling bar musician getting a gig in the Madison Square Gardens. Never going to happen. "Of course, I know that gallery, I mean those galleries. Do you need me to be a cater waiter there or something for one of your galas?"

He snorted a little. "No, although I suppose you could do that. But, no, my partners and I would like to feature you in our upcoming show that centers around images from the music industry. I was quite impressed with your panels on ballerinas and musicians. I talked things over with my partners, and they're all in agreement. I need approximately 10 of your paintings delivered to me immediately. Choose among any of your paintings that center around the theme."

I almost fainted dead away right there. I blinked my eyes rapidly. "I'm so sorry, I thought you said that you wanted me to have a showing there."

"That's exactly what I am saying. Deliver those paintings to me by Wednesday of next week, please. The show will be in December, so you have a little over a month. If you compose any other paintings that fit the theme before the show, then I would need those as well."

And, just like that, he hung up.

I stood there, staring at the phone, feeling that I was dreaming. What? I was getting a showing at the best gallery in the city? Me? Goddamn, I never thought that something like that would happen for me. And just when I was ready to throw in the towel and head to Maine to work for my pop.

Shaking, I immediately called Dalilah. She picked up immediately. "Luke," she said. "My parents are here. We were just talking about you. Here, let me put my dad on."

"Oh, Dalilah, thanks, but can I talk to you for a few minutes first?"

"Of course. What's up?"

"You will never believe what just happened. Never in eleventy-millions years."

"What?" She sounded extremely eager to hear my news.

"Nottingham. He's giving me a showing at the Matthew Jane! The Matthew Jane, Dalilah! I mean, every art critic in town will be there. Art critics from around the world. Not to mention patrons and benefactors. Oh my god, I think I got my big break!"

By now, I was breathing heavily as the news started to sink in. If this goes well, I would be on my way. On my way to getting established internationally and maybe even becoming successful enough to make Dalilah my wife.

To my surprise, tears were streaking down my face, even though I rarely cried. When I found out that my mother was killed by a random mass shooter in a McDonald's ten years ago, that was the last time that I cried. And now I was really crying again.

I couldn't even hear Dalilah screaming, which she was, I

soon found out. "Luke, I don't believe it! I mean, I do believe it, because you so deserve it, but I can't tell you how happy I am! Oh, my god, this is the greatest news that I have ever heard. Ever!"

Both of us started laughing wildly, and I started to dance around the room. I just couldn't believe it. The gods were finally smiling upon me. Finally.

All at once, I couldn't wait to meet Dalilah's parents.

Chapter Twenty-Three

Dalilah delivered the suit to me by a courier, and I put it on. She was right. Her father and I were the exact same size. Weird, but that suit fit me like a glove. Of course, there was the issue of getting to the restaurant to meet them, and Dalilah insisted on sending a limo on her father's dime.

"Dalilah, I don't think that a limo will come here," I had said.

"Don't be silly. My father will pay that limo driver beaucoup, so trust me, the limo will come and get you. Be ready to meet the driver at 6."

So, I got ready and anxiously went downstairs right at six and, sure enough, there was a black limo waiting for me there on the street. I looked around, seeing that the homeless people with their shopping carts were looking at the limo like they hadn't quite seen anything like it before. One of them, Freddy, whistled when he saw me approaching.

"Ooooh, boy, Luke, you shine up like a brand new copper penny. Where you heading, boy?"

"Some fancy restaurant," I said with a smile. I gave the

guy the usual five bucks and patted him on the back. "Maybe I can sneak out a doggie bag for you, huh?"

"That would be great, but fancy restaurants don't do that."

I made a mental note to see if I could get something for Freddy, though. He was really a great guy, and he and I sometimes got into long discussions about our lives. Turns out that we had something in common – both of us had a parent who was murdered. Mine was in a mass shooting, while his dad was killed in a gang-related incident when he was only 2.

Shit like that can destroy a person. It didn't me, but Freddy had a hard life on top of that as well. I felt for him. *There, but for the grace of god go I.*

The limo driver got out and opened the door, and I stepped into the limo and sat down in the back.

I nervously twiddled my thumbs as the limo took me to Eleven Madison. I tried very hard to remember that Dalilah had mentioned, more than once, that her parents were very down to earth. But I couldn't help it. Nottingham – that was who I envisioned all rich men to be. Cold pricks. Of course, Dalilah had to be right when she said that her parents were different. After all, she had turned out pretty cool and down to earth herself. I doubted that she could have been as unpretentious as she was if her parents weren't as well.

Finally, the limo pulled up to the restaurant, and I stepped out after the limo driver got out of the car and let me out. That was a strange thing for me, as well – having somebody escort me in and out of the car.

I stepped into the restaurant, which was gorgeous. Twenty foot tall ceilings, white walls, enormous windows, and cool hanging lanterns. Dalilah was already there with her parents, and she saw me immediately and came over to me. "Oh, Luke, you look so handsome. I mean, you always do, but, wow, you do clean up nice."

I smiled, knowing that she was right. Of course, it didn't hurt that I was wearing an Armani suit that fit like a glove. Strange how much her father and I were alike in height and build.

She escorted me over to her table, where her father was apparently drinking Scotch and her mother was sipping on a dirty martini. Her mom and dad both stood up when I got to the table, and her dad shook my hand. "Nice to meet you, Luke. I'm Ryan, and this is my wife, Iris." At that, her mom also stood up and shook my hand.

"Good to meet you, Luke." I shook her hand and kissed her on the cheek. She giggled a little bit, and everybody sat down.

Dalilah excitedly put her hands on my shoulders. "Well, dad, you are looking at the next international sensation in the world of art, Luke Roberts."

Dalilah's handsome father smiled broadly, and I felt at ease almost immediately. He raised his glass. "Well, cheers to that," he said, as we all clinked our glasses. "Tell me about the gig, Luke."

"Well, let's see. I apparently am going to get a showing at the Matthew Jane Gallery in Chelsea. Not entirely sure, but I understand that the gallery is featuring impressionistic portraits of musicians and ballerinas, and I happen to have many works centered on that theme, and I guess I'm going to be a part of that show."

Ryan raised his eyebrows. "Matthew Jane. Wow. You really went from zero to hero, huh?" And then he smiled as Dalilah shot him a dirty look. "That came out wrong. At any rate, congratulations on that. That will be a tremendous boost to your career, no doubt."

I looked down at my plate, which already had an appetizer on it. This place was one of those places where there were tiny portions of amazing things, and this appetizer was delicious. It was sweet bread, which I understood was some kind of pancreas of an animal. Dalilah also had one, and her parents, being vegan, opted for a small cup of corn chowder. "I hope you don't mind," Dalilah said. "I really wanted you to try this sweet bread. If you don't like it, we can send it back."

"No, actually, this is delicious," I said, taking a bite. And, indeed it was.

"Dalilah tells me that you're a fabulous artist," her mother, Iris, was saying. "I'd love to see your work in person. I mean, I saw it on the website, and it is absolutely brilliant. It kinda reminds me, somewhat, of some of the stuff that Ryan did when he was young and bold."

Ryan shrugged. "It's a hobby now, but when I was your age, I really was quite serious about it. That's where Dalilah gets her artistic bent. Well, that and the fact that my mother is also an artist in a way. I mean, she's an opera singer, but she's also very creative in the mind. She's pretty left of center."

I nodded, remembering Dalilah telling me that Maggie, her grandmother, was a schizophrenic who has it under control. Maggie apparently lived in Kansas City, although it was my understanding that she was going to possibly be moving to New York to stay in Dalilah's parents' guest house. Ryan apparently was worried that she might go off her meds again, which she did before, to disastrous consequences.

Throughout the evening, the parents asked me questions that weren't too probing. I really did start to feel comfortable with them after a little while, especially after having a couple of scotches with her dad. At his insistence. I wasn't much of a scotch guy. I really wasn't a hard alcohol guy, period, preferring to stick to beer. But the scotch was smooth as silk, and went down well, so I didn't mind having a couple of neat scotches with Ryan.

I ended up the evening really having enjoyed myself. I felt much more confident talking about myself, now that I finally had something to talk about. I had to admit that I was feeling validated. Completely validated by this offer that Nottingham had made out of the clear blue sky. I actually started to feel that I was somebody. That alone gave me confidence.

Finally, the evening was over, and there were hugs all around with everyone. The parents were going to Dalilah's apartment to meet her there, but Dalilah wanted to go with me in the limo to make sure that I got home okay. I was more than willing to share my limo with her.

We ended up going to the Shake Shack for strawberry milkshakes on the way home, and I also ordered a burger and fries to go, as I had promised Freddy that I would bring him something, and there wasn't anything on the Eleven Park tasting menu that was suitable for him. But I knew how much Freddy liked his burgers and fries.

Finally, I arrived home. I so wanted to invite her up, but I knew that she had to get home to see her parents, who would be waiting for her. So, I kissed her passionately in the limo, and her body responded eagerly.

"I think that things just might be turning around for me, Dalilah. At least, I hope so. I want to give you the world, and I hope to be able to through my art. That would be the dream."

"You will be able to, Luke. This opportunity is huge. I mean, it couldn't be bigger. Once the critics and the patrons see your work, you won't be able to work fast enough to satisfy them. You're going to get the attention and acclaim that you deserve. And at such a young age, too. I knew that you would, Luke. I had no doubt. I told you to believe in yourself, because I really believe in you."

"I know you do, Dalilah. I love you, Dalilah. I really do."

"I love you too, Luke."

I kissed her again, wanting the kiss to go on forever. I wanted to do so much more with her, and I might have, if she didn't have to get home.

For once, I was starting to see a glimmer of hope that I might be good enough for her. Everything was finally coming together. I was going to get a huge platform to show myself to the world, and Dalilah was going to be mine. I could feel it.

We were going to be together.

Chapter Twenty-Four

Dalilah

I was so excited for Luke, I was practically bouncing off the walls. I just couldn't believe that Nottingham decided, all on his own, to give Luke a gig. It just goes to show that I probably should have had more faith and patience, instead of trying to meddle the way that I was.

And Luke...my parents loved him, that was plain. My mom was giggling like a schoolgirl about the jokes that Luke was telling, and he and my dad really did have a ton in common. Not just the fact that they are both artistic, but they also seemed to see the world in much the same way. Luke surprisingly knew a lot about my father's passion, animal rights, and was able to engage him at length about different aspects of animal treatment. And, of course, my mom has the same passion, so the three of them talking about this topic took up much of the conversation. But I could tell that all three of them were getting along quite well.

When he kissed me in the limo, one thing was for sure – I didn't want to stop. I wanted, so badly, for him to invite me up to his apartment and ravage me. And I think that is exactly what would have happened if I didn't have to get back home to see my parents. They had a hotel room again, as the house in Montauk wouldn't be ready to move into until Sunday. But I knew that they wanted to talk to me one on one some more. Especially after meeting Luke – I suppose that they really needed a post-mortem, so to speak.

I got back into my apartment, and my parents were both sitting on the floor, teasing each other. My dad was tickling my mom, and she was on the floor giggling and yelling at him to stop.

"Huh, Iris, you want me to stop, do you? Well, you know the magic word."

She was laughing so hard that she could barely get the word out – Amsterdam. Then he stopped, as that word apparently meant something to the two of them. But he was still laughing, and so was she.

They saw me and both of them stood up, a look of mirth still on both of their faces. "Dalilah," my mother said. "Ryan and I were talking about that wonderful boy. Where did you find him?"

"He's doing an art project. A portrait of me." I didn't mention that it was a nude. My parents didn't quite know that I did that, unless blabbermouth Nick clued them in, as he no doubt knew about my nude modeling from Nottingham. I kind of wanted to keep that part of my life from my parents.

"Well, he has a real future," my father was saying. "Especially if he's getting a major gig this early in his career. Anyhow, your mom and I are very happy that you have finally found somebody. We were getting very worried about you."

Then he paused, and I knew what was coming next.

I was right.

"That said, Dalilah," dad was saying. "Nick told me that you are also dating an older man whom he considers to be somewhat dangerous for you. I'm not one to judge others' lifestyles, but I really hope, Dalilah, that you aren't getting into BDSM. That can be very destructive if you don't know what you're doing and you don't understand that way of life."

Both my mom and dad were just staring at me, hoping for me to reassure them that I hadn't gone that route.

I didn't really know what to say. So, I told them the truth. As shitty as the truth was.

"Oh, god. Now, I know what you're going to say after I tell you this. 'Dalilah, we raised you better than this. You shouldn't use people.' So, I already know that I shouldn't use others, so, please, spare me the inevitable lecture."

My mother raised an eyebrow. "Not liking where this is going. But go ahead."

So, I told them the entire story.

My dad took a deep breath and said "so you're only dating Nottingham because you want him to help Luke. Sounds like that was unnecessary, if you didn't really have to talk him into featuring Luke. Nottingham evidently came up with that on his own."

"Yes, that's ironic. But, it means that I can stop seeing Nottingham now. That's good, right?"

My mom shook her head. "Dalilah, Dalilah, Dalilah. I know you don't want to hear it, but what are you thinking? People are not on this earth for you to manipulate as you wish. This is a fine kettle of fish that you have gotten yourself into. A fine kettle of fish."

I looked down at the floor, ashamed. To think that I was felt like I was turning over a new leaf. Trying to be a better person. Yet, I ended up doing something shitty and, it turns out, unnecessary. And Alaina was right – I was in over my head. I had no idea how Nottingham was going to react when he found out that I didn't want to see him anymore.

I had dug myself into a hole, and I knew that I had to keep on seeing Nottingham until Luke got his show. I didn't know for sure, but Nottingham might do something stupid like pull Luke's show, if he was really upset with me. After all, it was I who brought the subject of Luke up to him in the first place. He might pull Luke's show just to spite me.

If my mom and dad could read my mind, and see that I was going to keep on using Nottingham for the next month or so, they would have blown a gasket.

"I did it for a good cause," I said weakly. But, judging by the looks on both my parents' faces, they were unconvinced, to say the very least.

"No cause is good when it comes to toying with people's emotions, Dalilah," my dad was saying. "And you are right. We *did* raise you better than this."

I looked at my mom, steaming. How dare she put the guilt trip on me, when she left dad when she was pregnant with me and didn't even tell him until I was like four months old. Once again, I questioned how any of them, including Nick, could have any kind of moral authority.

Then I calmed down as I thought about the fact that it is their job as parents to try to keep their children from making the same mistakes that they did. They did stupid stuff in their youth, and they no doubt drew the line when I wanted to do similar stupid stuff.

"So, what am I supposed to do?" I asked them. "I got myself into this. How do I get myself out?"

"Come clean," my dad said. "Tell Nottingham the truth, and let the chips fall where they may."

"Oh, no. No. That will get Luke's show pulled for sure. No. There is no way that I'm going to put his future in jeopardy just because I made a huge mistake. And you can't ask me to do that."

My mom just sighed and shook her head. She looked sad. "Well, Dalilah, I suppose it's a case of inexperience and youth getting in your way. God knows your father and I have made worse mistakes than this when we were your age. So, yeah, there's nothing that can really be done here. Just please get away from that Nottingham man before he does something to hurt you."

I was quiet, not wanting to tell them that I felt that I had to carry out my relationship with Nottingham until Luke had his show. I didn't want to leave anything to chance. I mean, Nottingham probably wouldn't pull Luke's show just because I dumped him, but he might. He might, knowing that I was Luke's advocate. He seemed unstable that way.

I desperately wanted to change the subject. "So, dad, what did you really think about Luke's art work? I know that you've had the chance to really look at it on his website."

"Very original stuff. He has taken elements of some of the best influences in his genre and put his own spin on it. So, his work is fresh, yet represents the best of the modern impressionistic movement. His show really should be a hit, especially if it is going to center around his paintings on the ballerinas. Those are magnificent."

I nodded my head. "I think so, too. I don't see how his show won't be a hit."

My parents and I, once again, talked into the early morning. They told me about what was going on with their animal rights foundation, and I told them as much about my life was I was willing to share with them. Which meant that I admitted to feeling lonely and isolated, and I also told them how Luke brought me out of that. How he was bringing me back into the living, and had awakened a passion in me for life.

I didn't tell them that Luke had also awakened a passion in me for other things, but I didn't think that it was necessary to tell them that. I hated discussing such intimate matters with my parents.

My mother kissed me on my forehead. "Dalilah, we're so happy that you finally found somebody. Especially as somebody as kind and seemingly even-tempered as Luke. He seems to be your artistic and intellectual equal, as well, and I know how important that is to you. So, we're happy. Don't do anything to mess it up, though, like continuing to see Nottingham as well."

I took a deep breath, not telling her the truth, which was that I was going to continue to sneak around with Nottingham. Just until the show was underway and Luke got his acclaim. Then I would let Nottingham down gently.

Dumb strategy, but one that I had to see through.

I was in it, and I had no idea how to get out of it.

Chapter Twenty-Five

Luke and I had turned a corner in our relationship, after he got the gig with Nottingham's gallery. I came over to his apartment to help him pick out the paintings that he was going to show. He had some of the paintings there, and some were at a storage locker. But we picked out the very best ones, and he delivered it to Nottingham personally.

We also were hanging out a lot together. I wanted to be with him always, which was a problem, because he worked a lot. So, when he was working at the bar, I stayed home and painted. I was getting better, and starting to like my work again. I still wasn't ready to show it to the world, or even to Luke, but just creating in and of itself was making me feel so much better about everything.

Of course, I was also doing my nude modeling gigs for other artists, because I had to eat. Nottingham was paying me $1000 a week to pose for Luke, though, so that helped. He clarified that for me the first week – that the $1000 sitting fee was a weekly one. So, I didn't have to take nearly as many side jobs, and I quit the job at the school altogether.

That was only paying $25 an hour, which wasn't worth it anymore.

But, Luke and I hung out as much as we could. Generally, he came to my apartment and we got take-out and continued our card games. Which would end up in make-out sessions, inevitably. We couldn't keep our hands off of each other, no matter how much we tried.

I snuck out with Nottingham once a week as well, usually when Luke was working. Nottingham and I did stuffy things like going to his fancy rich dude's club, and things like that, while Luke and I went bowling, played cards, went to the Shake Shack and Joey's Diner, and I smoked him at the pool hall more than once.

"You're a shark, Dalilah," Luke complained as I sunk the fourth ball in a row. I was on my way to running the table. I couldn't help it. I was a genius, so I saw the geometric patterns that I needed to hit the balls in just the right places. And I was just too competitive in pool to possibly try to let Luke win.

But Luke was gracious about my pool skills, as he was about everything else. "Aw, you beat me here at the pool hall. Let's see how you do with b-ball down at the court tomorrow. I think I'll school you there."

And, indeed he did. I was good on the basketball court, but Luke was phenomenal, sinking basket after basket. He played good defense, too. He took no prisoners, which I appreciated, and he didn't let up, either. He ended up schooling me, 20-10, but getting 10 points on him was pretty damned good, considering how good his defense was.

He smiled his crooked smile as he did a little dance around the court. "I schooled you, I schooled you, I schooled you. I.schooled.you," he said, pointing to me.

So, I tackled him down to the ground, and the two of us

wrestled on the playground, laughing. He kissed me, and got on top of me, but we stopped when a bunch of little kids came onto the court, ball in hand, and said "get a room. We need the court."

Which was just as well, as it started to lightly snow again. Luke and I got on the bus and headed to his apartment.

He made me some hot chocolate, and we sat on the floor, our backs to his futon. "Love this hot chocolate recipe," he said. "The secret is chili pepper and cardamom. Interesting, huh? Wakes up your taste buds."

"That it does," I said. I took some of the whipped cream off the top of the cup of cocoa and put it on his nose. He smiled as he rubbed his nose on my nose, and then he licked the whipped cream off of it.

"Mmmm, you taste good," he said. "I wonder why?"

I started laughing. "Of course I taste good. I have whipped cream on my nose, dummy!"

He kissed my lips and bit my upper lip lightly. "No, I'm pretty sure that it's just you that tastes good. Not the whipped cream. Too sweet for my taste."

"Oh," I whispered. "You want a piece of this?" I asked, putting my wrist up to his mouth. He started sucking on it hungrily. Then he put his lips to my neck, and started kissing my neck and clavicle.

I put my arms around his lean frame and pulled him down on top of me on the floor. I spread my legs underneath him, and he put one of his legs in between mine. He put his elbows on either side of my head, and he hovered above me. He kissed my forehead and I sighed.

God, I wanted this. I wanted this more than I had ever wanted anything in my entire life. He was such an amazing kisser, and he felt so incredibly warm on top of me. Which was a good thing, because the heat was on low, and the night air outside was starting to dip. I looked out the window briefly, and snow was really starting to fall.

I thought about how glorious it would be to be stranded right there in that apartment with Luke. With nothing for us to do but explore each other's bodies languidly and slowly.

He was still on top of me, so I unbuttoned the top part of his jeans. As I unzipped them, he started breathing heavily, and kissed me again, full on the lips. I rubbed his penis, which was still behind his underwear, and he groaned lightly.

"Please, do it, Dalilah. Oh, my god. You don't know how much I want this. You have no idea."

"I think that I know," I said. "Because I want this just as much."

At that, I brought his jeans down completely, and his underwear, and I started to stroke him up and down. He had a very nice dick. Large, but not overly so. It seemed perfect for me.

He was still partially clothed, at least his torso was. He was wearing his t-shirt, and he took it off so that he was completely naked. He then sat down on the floor, his back against the couch. He looked so perfect, just like I knew that he would. Long, lean, with perfectly sculpted muscles on his pecs and abs.

I put my hands on his sculpted chest, and rubbed it while I kissed him on his lips. He put his hands in my hair, and then started to kiss my neck. "Oh, Dalilah," he said. "Can I please take off your top?"

I nodded my head wordlessly, and he slowly took off my t-shirt. I unhooked my bra and let it fall to the floor. Then I unzipped my own jeans and took them off, along with my socks and shoes.

Breathing heavily, I laid down on the blanket that was on the floor, and he hovered above me. Then he laid on top of me, and started kissing my breasts. Between my legs, I could feel his hard-on, just at the edge of my opening. He also started to kiss my neck, and he lightly started stroking my breasts with his hands. He was so gentle, and I could feel the goosebumps forming on my skin. My entire body was flushing and feeling warm, and I could feel my nipples harden as he lightly bit and sucked each one.

He fingered my vagina lightly, and I started to groan as I felt his fingers inside of me swirling. He kissed me from my navel and ended up tonguing me lightly between my legs. The pleasurable sensation that had begun in my body was starting to burst, and, out of the blue, I could feel every part of my body just start to feel as if it was on fire.

I couldn't believe what I was feeling as Luke was slowly sucking and licking inside of me. This was unlike any feeling that I ever had before. I started to squirm, because the feeling was so strong and so pleasurable.

Then he was back to kissing my lips passionately. I wanted him inside of me so badly. I had never wanted anything so much in my entire life.

"Luke, please, please, please. Please make love to me," I said.

So, he entered me slowly. I immediately started crying out, because, if what I was feeling before when he was tonguing my clit was powerful, this feeling was out of this world. He was filling me up, slowly and sensually, and it was almost torture to feel how strong the pleasurable sensation really was.

He kissed my lips again as he slowly and surely stroked himself in and out, in and out. I put my hands on his strong back, and pulled a little bit on his hair. And then I got on my side, and he entered me from behind. This brought me to orgasm once more. He was behind me, his hands on my breasts. He moved his hands down more towards my waist, and I turned my head and he devoured my lips with his.

I could hear his heart pounding in my ears, and I could feel my heart pounding along with the beat of his. It felt like my entire body was pulsating wildly with every thrust. He started to pick up speed, and then I could feel him pulsating inside of me. He groaned mightily, and then, with both of us breathing heavily, and his body wrapped around mine, he pulled out.

For a few minutes, the two of us just laid there on the blanket, not really knowing what to say for once. He took a tendril of my hair, and whisked it away from my face, and kissed my forehead lightly. "Oh, Dalilah, you just don't know what you do to me."

"How could I not know? Because you do the same to me."

He stroked my cheek, and kissed me again. "I just feel like I'm dreaming. You are the woman that has been my muse for this long, and I never thought that it was possible that we could be together. But we are. We are, and we will be. I just know that I can give you the moon, the stars and the world, Dalilah. Everything in the universe, I can give that to you. I know that now, and it feels amazing."

"It does, Luke, it does feel amazing. I know, too, that you can give me everything that you feel that I need. But I could never convince you that I really don't need anything but you. Only you. We could live on the streets together like Freddy, and I would be just as happy, as long as I'm with you."

"I wish that I knew that you meant that," he said. "At any rate, it doesn't matter, because, with this showing, I'll literally be on my way. On my way, Dalilah, to being able to give you all that you could ever want or need."

At that, he kissed me again, and I could feel him growing once more. I spread my legs open again, and he was, once again, thrusting inside of me. This time he was a little more urgent, just a tad more rough. I came to yet another orgasm, and so did he.

We sat up and drank our hot cocoa some more, although, by then, it was just cocoa. It wasn't hot at all. I could taste the spices much better at that point. It reminded me of Luke, really – sweet, but also spicy. I really enjoyed drinking it, almost as much as I enjoyed drinking in Luke. His essence had become a part of me.

As the snow fell outside, Luke and I kept each other warm for the rest of the night. We couldn't get enough of each other, as we made love for the rest of the night in a slow and deliberate fashion.

The next day, I reluctantly left Luke's apartment, because he had to be at work, and I was greeted to around six inches of snow on the sidewalk, it occurred to me that life was finally at its pinnacle. After my slow decline during my years when I had such mental blocks, combined with my depression, I thought that life was never going to be good again.

Now, after having spent the night of my life with the man of my dreams, life suddenly seemed to be not just colorful, but on fire. When I got back to my apartment, I immediately took to my canvas and painted something that, when I finished it six hours later, I *knew* was good. There wasn't any doubt in my mind this time. It came from my heart, it came from my passion, and it was inspired by Luke himself.

I was finally back.

Chapter Twenty-Six

For the next few weeks, I continued to play my increasingly dangerous game. I felt that I had to keep Nottingham satisfied, just enough that he wouldn't throw a tantrum and pull Luke's show. I was so paranoid about that happening, and I had to prevent that by any means possible. So, I continued to see Nottingham a few times a week. I never brought up Luke to him, ever, because the last thing that I wanted was for Nottingham to be suspicious.

But Luke and I had finally gotten to the point where we were in a real, honest to god, relationship. I started to spend more and more of my time at his apartment, because that was easier for us, as he was working a lot. That way, I could hang out at his place while he was working, and I could spend much more time with him. While he pulled his shifts, I hung out in his place and painted and read and just generally was productive. My work was getting better and better, I knew that. Luke was also very impressed with the stuff that I was composing while he was downstairs tending bar.

"Wow, Dalilah, you really got your voice back," he said,

as he admired one of my paintings that was an absolutely riotous mélange of colors and shapes. It was a cityscape and a subway, but this was hidden in the geometric shapes that surrounded these forms. "I'm so impressed with you. I guess it's like a bicycle, huh? It never leaves you."

"Well, it helps that I'm so inspired these days. Inspired by you."

"Nah, you're just inspired because you're getting properly laid," he said with a wink. "Speaking of which...."

I shook my head. "Uh, uh, uh," I said, shaking my finger at him. "Not now. We have to eat. I have some wonderful gourmet spaghetti and meatballs cooking, and it will be cold if we get to our usual marathon sex sessions."

But, of course, while I stood behind his ancient stove, wearing nothing but one of his button-downs and socks, Luke came up to me and put his hands on my breasts. He kissed the back of my neck, and then put me up on the counter behind us. He kissed me passionately, and fingered me, and then brought down his pants and thrust into me while I sat on the counter with my legs wrapped around him. I didn't even think about the sanitary nature of what we were doing on his counter. He felt so fucking amazing, all I could think about was the powerful orgasm that I was feeling as he thrust in and out of me while I sat on the counter.

Finally, he came inside of me, and he kissed me on my forehead. "See, we can do quickies, too. Now get to the dinner, wench. I'm hungry."

After dinner, which we usually ate on the coffee table, both of us sitting on the floor, Luke casually said "what do you say we go ice-skating this Saturday? We'll be with the other hoards of people in front of the Rockefeller Center. It'll be fun!"

I giggled. "I've never been ice-skating."

"Never? How is that possible?"

"I don't know, it just was something that I've never done."

"Well, looks like this is one more thing that I can school you on, because, my friend, you are looking at a long-time hockey player. I played since I was a kid. I'll have to show off my moves for you, so you can ooh and ah over me." And then he smiled. "Seriously, I'd love to teach you to skate. I really did play hockey since I was about four years old, so it's something that I'm really good at and I love to teach others."

I smiled, imagining Luke on the hockey rink. "Were you any good?"

"Our teams usually went to the championships. I was always a starting forward."

"You didn't play hockey," I said, teasingly. "You couldn't have. You have all your teeth. And what beautiful straight teeth they are."

"Dentures," he said. "No, really, you don't see me taking them out at night and put them in a glass jar. Don't freak out if you get up in the middle of the night and see my teeth there in the bathroom."

I looked at him, not knowing if he was joking or not. But, he soon burst out laughing, so I started laughing as well.

"Nah," he said. "I got lucky. I stayed out of fights, or tried to. Anyhow, we had a really good enforcer who took the brunt of the fights for the rest of us. Now that guy probably is missing more than a few teeth." He shook his head. "Man, that guy was enormous. And powerful. He was the best enforcer in the league."

"Enforcer? Is that like a body guard?"

"Something like that. It's a guy who responds to the other team's aggressiveness, and either fights them or checks them. So, when you go to a fight and some hockey breaks out, you're usually watching two enforcers going at it."

"I see," I said. "Oh, what I have missed out on growing up in the Midwest. We don't get into hockey like you Northeasterners do."

"You have missed out on a lot. Hockey is really a beautiful game if you think about it. I mean, it's fast and aggressive, of course, but it takes so much athleticism and skill. Much more so than most of the other sports." He shrugged. "Well, that's it. I'm just going to have to show you by taking you to a Rangers' game. You'll thank me later."

"Hmmm, how about I thank you now?" I said, as I unbuttoned his pants. He groaned as my lips hungrily found his enormous erection, and I sucked him greedily. He put his hands underneath my shirt again, and brought me down on top of him.

As he stroked my back, and kissed my lips, he said "I love you, Dalilah. I love you more than I thought it was possible to love anybody. Marry me, Dalilah. Be my wife."

"Yes," I said. "Yes, I'll marry you. Yes. Yes. Yes."

Perhaps it was said in the heat of passion, but I knew that my saying yes came from my heart. Because I was feeling that way about him, and had been ever since he kissed me in my apartment that one night.

That night, after we made love several more times, Luke said "oh, Dalilah, that just came out. I mean, I do want to marry you. But that wasn't the proper way to ask you at all. Can I have a mulligan?"

"Of course," I said. "Of course. After all, we can't very well tell our kids that you asked me to marry you while we were fucking. That wouldn't be right."

He started laughing at that. "No, it wouldn't be right at all." And then he kissed me and once again was inside of me. "But I do love fucking you, Dalilah. I do love that very much."

"I do too."

Chapter Twenty-Seven

It was on the ice rink, that Saturday, when everything started going wrong. Luke and I had a great time. His show was coming up in a few more weeks, so he felt on top of the world, and so did I.

He skated rapidly around the rink, while I stood in the middle, wanting just to stay up. He was showing off for me, of course. I loved him for that, too. He had such a boyish way about him, really. He leaped up in the air, and, to my surprise, he was able to execute a perfect turn in the air. He must have executed three revolutions before landing softly on the ice.

As he skated towards me, a huge smile on his perfect face, I stood there looking at him, my arms crossed in front of me. I pretended to be annoyed by his antics, but, really, I was just charmed by them. "You think that's cool, huh? That you're some faggy figure skater? Here I thought you were just a macho hockey dude. What's up with that?"

At first he looked crestfallen, but then he saw the smile on my face creeping up. "Sorry, Dalilah, I just wanted to demonstrate to you how I feel. I don't know where I learned how to do a triple jump, but it's something that I think that I do well."

"Along with a multitude of other things," I said. "And you know what those are, I'm quite sure."

"I do," he said. "I do, I do, I do." And then, at that, he got down on one knee. "Dalilah Gallagher, I told you that I had to do this properly, so that we could have a memorable story to tell to our kids." He produced a box and he opened it. A perfect diamond ring was in there, and I knew that it had to set him back a bundle. My hand flew involuntarily to my mouth, as I looked at the perfect little diamond, which was princess cut and set in gold.

He looked at me earnestly, his breath visible in the cold air. "You have made me happier than anybody has ever made me in my life. I couldn't imagine life without you. Dalilah Gallagher, would you please do me the honor of being Mrs. Roberts for the rest of your life?"

I nodded my head, tears running down my cheeks. "Yes, yes, yes, yes, yes. One thousand times yes!"

At that, he stood up, and kissed me. There were people all around, pointing at us and smiling. Several of them started clapping and cheering.

He slipped the ring on my finger, and I looked at it in awe. I looked at him. "How did you…"

He shrugged. "I pawned my guitar." And then he started laughing when he saw my shocked expression. "Don't worry, I'm going to get a new one when I sell out of that Matthew Jane show. And then I'm going to buy you the best wedding ring I can find."

"Oh, Luke, this ring is so beautiful. It really is. I love it. I love it so much."

"Well, it doesn't compare to your mom's red diamond

ring. I've never seen anything like that. Ever. But, this comes from my heart."

"I love it. And I love you." Truth be told, he could have literally gotten me a Cracker Jack ring, and I would have been just as happy. Because the ring came from the heart.

We skated that day for hours, after Luke patiently showed me how to stroke on the ice. At first, it was awkward, as I fell many times, always in his arms. But, by the end of the day, I was tentatively stroking around the ice with him. I never had a better day.

That day was the pinnacle. It really was. Especially considering what was to come. My behavior with Nottingham was not to be without consequences, I soon found.

And those consequences were things that I never, ever imagined.

Chapter Twenty-Eight

The Wednesday after Luke and I got engaged, I had a date with Nottingham. I was so looking forward to the day when I didn't have to see him anymore, because Luke would have his show, and the critics would love him, and he would get a multitude of benefactors just fighting over him. Of that, I was sure. So, after this show, he wouldn't need Nottingham.

In the meantime, though, he did. So, I had to keep Nottingham happy.

As I was falling more and more in love with Luke, it was soooo difficult to be with Nottingham. It was always hard to put on an act for him, and it was increasingly getting more difficult. But act I did. I felt like I should have been up for the Academy Award. *And the Oscar goes to Dalilah Gallagher for her role in Dates with Nottingham!*

He picked me up in his limo, as usual. I got in, and proceeded to kiss him lightly on the lips.

He kissed me back, but I could tell that there was something really wrong. I could sense it.

"It's good to see you, Dalilah," he said. "As always."

"You too, Blake. Where are we going?"

"I thought that we could just drive around a little bit, and see the city."

"Sounds like fun to me."

He didn't say anything more for several minutes. Then he said "Luke Roberts. I know about the two of you."

My heart started racing. NO! NO! PLEASE GOD NO!

As casually as possible, feeling the lump in my throat, I said "I'm sorry? I mean, of course you know about us. I've been posing for him for months now."

He leered at me, and then slapped me hard across the face. "Fucking cunt bitch liar. How stupid do you think that I am?"

My hand went up to where he just slapped me, and I felt tears coming down my face. "I don't know what you're talking about!"

"You and he. Him on one knee on the ice rink. Any of that ringing a bell?"

Oh, shit. Crap. Crap. Crap. "Blake, I don't know what to say."

"I do. His show is going to be cancelled. And he's finished in this town. Nobody will touch him now, after I get through with him." And then he gave me a very cruel look. "Really, Dalilah. Seeing me just so that I could give Luke a showing. I would have done that all on my own. You never had to manipulate me like that. But you did. You did, and I'm going to punish you by pulling your boyfriend's show."

"No, no, no, no, no please. Please, Blake, please don't do this to him. Please. Please. It wasn't his fault. He had no idea about you and me. Please don't take this out on him. Please, Blake, please."

I started to panic. Luke's opportunity of a lifetime would not only be slipping through his fingers, but

Nottingham had the power to blackball Luke from further shows.

There must be something I can do. Something, anything. Anything. Anything at all. Anything.

"You can't do this. He needs this. He needs this. Please, Blake, please don't do this. Please."

He slapped me again, harder this time. "Shut up, cunt."

And then he looked out the window. I crawled towards him, tugging desperately on his jacket sleeve. "Blake, please. Please don't. I'll do anything. Anything at all. Whatever you want. Whatever you want. Just please don't pull his show. Please."

"Anything?"

"Anything."

"Okay, then. You'll be my wife. You will never see that boy again. And you will submit to me, whatever I want, whenever I want. I can beat you, in the context of our sex games, of course, and you can't say one thing. That's what I want. I want you to be my wife, and I want you to be my sex slave."

Without thinking, I just said "I do this, and Luke still gets his show?" That was literally all that I could think about at that moment. I didn't have time to think about how devastated I was going to be acquiescing to his terms. I only wanted to make sure that Luke got his show. That was all I could see.

"Yes, Luke will get his show. I'll make sure that every top critic and benefactor in the city will be there, too. Luke will be a superstar, there is no doubt in my mind."

"And if I don't agree to your terms?"

He shrugged. "Luke's show gets pulled and I'll use my considerable power to make sure that he never gets a show in this town, ever."

I took an enormous breath. I had no choice. Nottingham held all the cards. Alaina's voice rang in my ears *don't be surprised if the manipulated becomes the manipulator, Dalilah. You're getting in over your head.*

It all came back to bite me at last.

Defeated, I said, quietly, "okay. I'll meet your terms."

He smiled wickedly. "I knew you would."

There was nothing more to say.

Next in the Fearless series

vinci-books.com/secrets-lies

**She gave up everything for his future, but now she's
risking it all for love.**

Dalilah Gallagher made the ultimate sacrifice, walking away from
the love of her life, Luke Roberts, to secure his dreams. Now,
trapped in a loveless marriage with the obsessive Nottingham, she
realizes her grave mistake. As Nottingham's twisted desires
escalate, threatening to destroy everything Dalilah holds dear, she
must find the strength to break free from his suffocating grasp.

Turn the page for a free preview…

Secrets & Lies: Chapter One

Dalilah

Today would be the worst day of my life. Bar fucking none. I would have to break the heart of the kindest boy that I have ever known, and the one person in this world who has been able to bring out my absolute best. All because of my fucking stupidity. I had the best of intentions, of course. I mean, I would like to think that I wouldn't have done what I did without having a good cause behind it. But no matter. The outcome was more tragic than I ever could have imagined. And the outcome was really all that mattered.

Already, Luke had called me and texted me excitedly about my coming over. I had begged off posing for him in the morning, texting him that I had a migraine headache and didn't want to be disturbed.

He texted me back: "Let me bring over a cold compress for your head. My mom used to get them, I know just what to do."

My heart was in my throat, and tears were streaming down my face as I texted: "Thanks, but I need to be alone right now. In a dark room." And that was all. I didn't want to lead him on, so I didn't put my usual "xoxoxoxo" at the end of my text.

He texted back a frowny face and "45683968," which was our secret code for "I love you." The numbers corresponded with the letters I-L-O-V-E-Y-O-U on our phone pads.

I shook my head, willing myself not to text him "45683968" right back. Willing myself not to tell Nottingham to go to hell, and not to go over to Luke and just let him hold me in his arms. That was what I was absolutely craving at this time.

No, Dalilah, you can't do that. You can't ruin him like that. If I had a moment of weakness, then that would be it. Luke would have his show pulled and he would be absolutely finished. That wouldn't be fair to him. I would be the instrument of his ruin. I couldn't look myself in the mirror if that ever happened. My life would be over, because I would have to live with the shame of knowing exactly what I caused with my manipulative ways.

Was this the lesser of two horrible evils? This was my Sophie's Choice, a choice between two unbearable options. One option was to break the heart of the man that I was indelibly in love with, a man that I felt that I would love until I died. There was something so powerful, so raw, about my feelings for him. We had only known one another a relatively short period of time, but he had already claimed me in a way that I never thought that I could be. My heart, my body, my soul — all belonged to him. As crazy as that sounded.

He made me finally believe. In soul mates. In the possibilities of true love. In the possibilities that there was something larger than oneself, and that sometimes sacrifices have to be made for the person that you should be destined to be with. And these sacrifices sometimes meant that you would have to live all your days apart from that person.

Which brought me to my other option. To break the heart of the man whom I was indelibly in love with. Which would happen if I didn't do as Nottingham wished. Because Luke would see his lifelong dream of becoming an artist of note slip through his fingers, and it would be doubtful that he would be able to recover from that. We would be together, but at what cost? At a cost to his career, his livelihood, his dream. How selfish would I be to let that happen?

This was definitely the only option. Break up with Luke, and do it in such a manner that he would be able to get over me quickly. Make him think that I had played him all along, and that I never actually cared about him at all. I had to do it. Any other way would mean that Luke would pine away for me instead of moving on with his life, which is what I wanted him to do. Needed him to do. Yes, I would be absolutely devastated and miserable without him. But I made my bed. I would have to live with the consequences of what I did, while freeing Luke to love again.

I briefly thought about telling Luke everything, so that he wouldn't be too terribly hurt. So that he could see that what I was doing was a necessary thing so that he could achieve his dreams. But, no. I knew that Luke would do one thing if I told him the truth – he would tell Nottingham to go to hell. I knew that boy well enough that I could see exactly what would happen if he knew the truth.

And I couldn't ever let that happen.

A new text was coming in. Luke was sending me a video of a cute little French Bulldog, my absolute favorite breed of dog, yapping, with the translation "I hear you are one sick puppy. Doggone it, get well soon."

I shook my head, wanting to scream out into the heavens. This was what I was going to be giving up. This goofy sense of humor that showed that Luke really got me. He knew just what to say and do to make me feel instantly better.

But there was no feeling better in this case. There couldn't be. Luke could never find the words and right video to make me feel better about what I had to do.

Nottingham called me. I picked up, dreading to talk to him. But I had to. I had to keep him perfectly happy. If I didn't, he would sabotage Luke's career. He had the absolute power to do so. Even after Luke had his show, Nottingham had the power to sabotage him. He also had the power to make Luke into the superstar that he was destined to be. He had all the best connections to make that happen for Luke.

After I had agreed to marry Nottingham, he showed me his plan for Luke, and I was astounded. The *Matthew Jane* was first, of course, and that would be the springboard for Luke to really start making a name for himself. Nottingham also wanted to show Luke at the *Galerie Emmanuel Perrotin* in Paris, for a spring showing. The *Emmanuel* was considered one of the hottest contemporary galleries in that city. The *Dominik Mares* in Prague would be next fall. Another world renowned contemporary art gallery. Nottingham wasn't personally involved with either of these galleries, yet he had the connections to get Luke a showing in each of them.

I knew what Nottingham was doing. He was simply

securing his investment, the investment being me. He knew that he had to sweeten the pot, to make sure that I didn't run for the exits when Luke's *Matthew Jane* showing was finished. And sweeten it, he did. Three major showings at three huge contemporary galleries, all in the span of a year? There was no way that Luke wouldn't end up on the A list after that.

"And Dalilah," he said to me, "don't think that you can leave me after Luke's *Matthew Jane* showing. I know you, and I know how devious you are. Trust me, I still have the power to destroy that boy at any point in his career. Even when he makes the A list. And I do say 'when,' not 'if.'"

I shrugged. I knew what he was saying was the truth. I was trapped. Sentenced to a loveless marriage that was actually much worse than merely being considered "loveless." It would be a destructive arrangement with us. Nottingham had the capacity for mental and physical abuse. I knew that.

I knew that, yet I had no choice in the matter. And it really didn't help when I repeated my mantra to myself, over and over again – that I was doing this for Luke. For him. For the man for whom I would walk through fire. Luke would have a wonderful life, filled with accolades and adoration. And, hopefully, he would find a woman to love and give him a family. I truly, truly hoped that Luke could move on without me and that he could be absolutely happy for the rest of his life. He so deserved that. If anybody in this world deserved it, it was him.

"Dalilah," Nottingham's stern voice addressed me through the phone. "Have you told him?"

"Not yet, Blake," I said.

"Tell him tonight. Tonight, Dalilah. Tonight, or our arrangement is off." At that, he simply hung up the phone.

That was how Nottingham rolled. He dispensed with pleasantries, like "hello," "goodbye," "please," and "thank you." Those words were the ones that the little people used, the ones who actually had a decent bone in their body.

Nottingham was the type of guy that, when somebody kindly opened the door for him, he would just buzz on through without even giving that person a second glance. He was the type of guy who would harangue a waitress for accidentally shorting him a dollar. He would call her stupid, right in front of me, and a cheat. He had more than one waitress in tears because of his behavior.

And I had to sit there and take it like a little wifey. At least, that would be what I would have to do from now on. I couldn't possibly get on Nottingham's bad side now. Not when he held Luke's future in his hands.

I looked forward to the day when, perhaps, Luke was enough of a superstar that he would no longer need Nottingham's largesse. Not that I would ever get back with Luke in that event. That would be too dangerous for him. I would always be paranoid that Nottingham just might have the power to pay a top critic to do to Luke what Henry Jacobs did to me – destroy his confidence to the point where he wouldn't be able to create anything. But, perhaps, I could at least get away from Nottingham one day.

That was my only dream.

Luke was texting me again. "Spaghetti and meatballs tonight and some pool down at the hall?"

I took a deep breath. This was, by far, going to be the very hardest thing that I had ever done in my life. I could think of nothing harder than breaking Luke's heart. I felt my tears rushing down my cheeks. It was starting to feel as if the tears never stopped, but that they were just incessant ever since Nottingham said those fateful words to me in his car – "Luke Roberts. I know about the two of you." Those words echoed in my ears, night and day, day and night.

I texted back.

"We need to talk."

Grab your copy...
vinci-books.com/secrets-lies